A PUFFIN BOOK

PROPERTY OF

Lula

ALF PRØYSEN was born in 1914 in Norway, where he became an important figure in literature, music, radio and television. The Mrs Pepperpot books first appeared in the 1950s and were an immediate success. They have been loved by children ever since and have been translated into many different languages. He died in 1970 at the age of fifty-six.

# ALF PRØYSEN

# MRS PEPPERPOT
## Strikes Again

*Illustrated by Björn Berg*

A PUFFIN BOOK

PUFFIN BOOKS

UK | USA | Canada | Ireland | Australia
India | New Zealand | South Africa

Puffin Books is part of the Penguin Random House group of companies
whose addresses can be found at global.penguinrandomhouse.com.

www.penguin.co.uk
www.puffin.co.uk
www.ladybird.co.uk

These stories were previously published in an omnibus edition of
*Mrs Pepperpot Stories* by Red Fox 2000
Reissued in this edition 2018

001

Set in 12.5/16.5 pt Sabon LT Std
Typeset by Jouve (UK), Milton Keynes
Printed and bound in Great Britain by Clays Ltd, Elcograf S.p.A.

A CIP catalogue record for this book is available from the British Library

ISBN: 978–0–241–36405–5

All correspondence to:
Puffin Books
Penguin Random House Children's
80 Strand, London WC2R 0RL

# Contents

*T*HERE *was once an old woman who went to bed at night as old women usually do, and in the morning she woke up as old women usually do. But one morning she found herself shrunk to the size of a pepperpot, and old women don't usually do that. The odd thing was, her name really was Mrs Pepperpot . . .*

# Mr Pepperpot and the Weather

MRS PEPPERPOT never listens to weather reports.

'If the sun shines I'm glad; if it rains I stay indoors,' she says.

But Mr Pepperpot listens to every single weather report both on TV and radio. He nods wisely when they talk about depressions over Dogger Bank or when the man on TV pushes arrows around to show where the troughs of high pressure are moving to.

'Just as I thought,' said Mr Pepperpot.

Not only that; he also remembered all the old country sayings about the weather, and all the traditional signs and portents. It wouldn't matter so much, thought Mrs Pepperpot, if he didn't always look for signs of *bad* weather. If Mr Pepperpot saw a holly tree full of red berries, he was sure the winter would be hard. If he heard thunder in September that meant storms at sea.

'More likely to be rats in the attic that you heard!' muttered Mrs Pepperpot.

Or he would say that it was foggy and that a foggy autumn brings a frosty Christmas.

'Try cleaning your spectacles!' said Mrs Pepperpot. 'You might get a clearer view.'

She was getting sick of all this moaning about the weather, and she decided to provide Mr Pepperpot with a *good* omen for a change.

If the fruit trees bloom in October, she'd heard him say, it meant the winter would be mild.

There was only one fruit tree in Mrs Pepperpot's garden, an old apple tree right outside the sitting-room window.

'Beggars can't be choosers,' she said, and she sat down to make apple blossom out of pink and white crepe paper. It took her all day, but at last she had a whole basketful of pretty pink and white flowers, which she hid in the outhouse.

Evening came and so did Mr Pepperpot. When she had given him his supper, Mrs Pepperpot fetched the basket of blossoms and hung it on as high a branch as she could reach. Then she started to climb up the tree herself.

But, of course, the inevitable happened; she SHRANK!

Luckily, she fell into the basket which swung on the branch, but didn't break it.

'Phew!' said Mrs Pepperpot, 'this is going to be hard work. If it had been daytime, I could have got the squirrel or the crow to help me; now I shall have to manage myself.'

Indoors Mr Pepperpot settled down in his armchair to watch TV. He had the radio on at the same time, in case he should miss any of the weather forecasts. So, while the TV was showing a film about girls in bikinis swimming in the warm South Seas under a blazing sun, the radio was telling Mr Pepperpot that a hailstorm was on its way to his area.

It was all very confusing, and Mr Pepperpot looked out of the window instead, just to see what the weather was *really* like.

What he saw made him blink; he couldn't believe his eyes! Out there in the garden the old apple tree was covered in pink and white blossom. Not only that, but more and more flowers kept

appearing and they even seemed to be moving –
creeping along the branches! Finally there was
just one flower moving; it was climbing up the
trunk of the tree, right to the topmost branch,
which seemed to bend towards the flower, then
bounce back with the flower attached like a
cheeky little flag at the top.

Mr Pepperpot was stunned. It was a miracle!
But just as he turned to call Mrs Pepperpot to

come and look, there was a sound of breaking branches and twigs, ending in a dull thud, like a sack of flour hitting the ground.

Mrs Pepperpot came through the door, holding her hand on her hip and limping a little.

'Where have you been?' asked Mr Pepperpot.

'Out,' said Mrs Pepperpot.

'What were you doing?' he asked.

'Coming in,' she answered.

'D'you know what?' said Mr Pepperpot. 'The old apple tree is in flower. Just come and see!'

They both looked out. But all was dark; there was not a sign of a pink and white blossom! They had all fallen off when Mrs Pepperpot fell out of the tree.

'You must have dreamed it,' said Mrs Pepperpot.

'But I saw it as clear as I see you now!' he declared. 'And it made me feel so happy to think we were going to have a mild winter.'

'You go right on thinking that, my dear,' said Mrs Pepperpot, 'stick to the good omens and leave the rest.'

And she went out into the garden and gathered up the paper flowers in her apron.

# Mrs Pepperpot in Hospital

MRS PEPPERPOT was in hospital.

Why? Well, you remember she fell out of that old apple tree when she was trying to make it blossom with paper flowers? After that her hip went on hurting for some time, so she went to the doctor, and he said she would have to go to hospital for X-rays, and stay overnight.

So there she was, in a nice clean hospital bed, lying next to a little girl called Rose who was going to have her tonsils out.

Rose was very unhappy. She was nearly seven years old, so it wouldn't do to cry, but she stuffed the sheet into her mouth and her little shoulders shook as she lay there with her back to Mrs Pepperpot.

'Can I do anything for you, pet?' she asked.

'Yes, please,' said the little girl stifling a sob. 'Could you tuck in my bedclothes?'

As Mrs Pepperpot went over to Rose's bed to tuck her up more comfortably, she SHRANK!

Rose was most surprised, because she thought the little old woman had disappeared. But Mrs Pepperpot called to her from the floor.

'I'm down here,' she shouted in her small voice.

'Goodness!' said Rose, looking over the edge of the bed. 'You must be Mrs Pepperpot!'

'Right first time!' said Mrs Pepperpot. 'And now it's your turn to help me.'

'What d'you want me to do?' Rose asked brightly, her tears quite forgotten.

'Pick me up in your hand and put me on your pillow,' said Mrs Pepperpot.

So Rose lifted her up.

'Fancy us two being in the same hospital,' she said.

'And in the same bed,' said Mrs Pepperpot, trying to make herself comfortable, but she kept slipping off the pillow.

'Haven't you got a box I could lie in?' she asked.

Rose brought out an empty chocolate box from her locker and made it up with a hankie for a sheet and her facecloth as a coverlet.

'Now we can pretend you are my little doll,' she said. 'That was why I was sad, because I hadn't brought my doll from home. But it doesn't matter when I have you to play with.'

First they played hide-and-seek, with Rose shutting her eyes while Mrs Pepperpot found clever places to hide all over the bed. Then they tried 'I spy' till Rose got tired and wanted to go to sleep.

She looked sad again, and when Mrs Pepperpot asked her what was the matter, she said:

'Mummy always sings to me before I go to sleep.'

'Oh,' said Mrs Pepperpot, 'that's easy! Just wait till you hear *my* song.'

This is what she sang:

> *'The Rose is white, the Rose is red,*
> *The Rose is now a sleepyhead.*
> *Soon she'll be as right as rain*
> *And play ring-a-roses with me again.'*

But then she couldn't remember any more, so she tried to think of something else with roses:

'If Moses supposes his toeses are roses, then Moses supposes erroniousleee . . .' she began, but stopped when she saw Rose's eyes were closing.

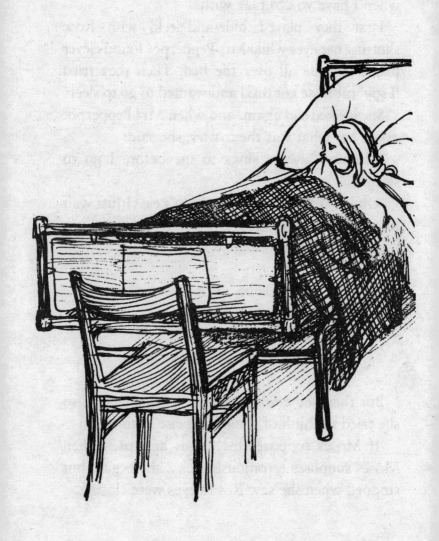

The little girl was not quite asleep. She turned her head a bit and murmured:

'I wish my pussy was here to lick my ear – he always does that before I go to sleep at home . . .'

Mrs Pepperpot looked around, but there was not much chance of finding even the smallest kitten in a hospital ward. So she thought of another idea. She took off her woolly nightcap and dipped it in the water glass on the table, and then she gently rubbed Rose's ear with it till she was fast asleep.

The door opened. It was the night sister coming in.

She came over to Rose's bed, but Mrs Pepperpot had popped into the chocolate box and covered herself with the facecloth and was lying as still as any doll.

'That's one child who doesn't miss her mother,' said the night sister, smiling down at Rose. 'She's sleeping like an angel – and so is her dolly.'

But when she turned round and found Mrs Pepperpot's bed empty, she rushed out of the ward shouting for the doctor. In a moment she was back, followed by two doctors and two nurses, all looking for Mrs Pepperpot, who by now, of course, had grown to her normal size and was lying in her own bed, as good as gold.

'Hullo,' said the chief doctor, 'the X-rays show your hip has mended, so you can go home tomorrow.'

'Thank you, doctor,' said Mrs Pepperpot. 'But what about little Rose?'

'Oh,' said the doctor, 'she'll be as right as rain!' and he walked out, followed by the rest of his staff.

'And play ring-a-roses with me again,' added Mrs Pepperpot, smiling at the sleeping Rose.

# Mrs Pepperpot's Christmas

O NE MORNING Mrs Pepperpot woke up and found she had shrunk. She climbed to the top of the bedpost and swung her legs while she wondered what to do.

'What a nuisance!' she said. 'Just when I wanted to go to the Christmas Market with Mr Pepperpot!'

She wanted to buy a sheaf of corn for the birds' Christmas dinner, and she wanted to get them a little bird house where she could feed them every day. The other thing she wanted was a wreath of mistletoe to hang over the door, so that she could wish Mr Pepperpot a 'Happy Christmas' with a kiss. But Mr Pepperpot thought this was a silly idea.

'Quite unnecessary!' he said.

But Mrs Pepperpot was very clever at getting her own way; so even though she was now no bigger than a mouse, she soon worked out a plan. She heard her husband put his knapsack down on the floor in the kitchen and she slid down the bedpost, scuttled over the doorstep and climbed into one of the knapsack pockets.

Mr Pepperpot put the knapsack on his back and set off through the snow on his kick-sledge, while Mrs Pepperpot peeped out from the pocket.

'Look at all those nice cottages!' she said to herself. 'I'll bet every one of them has a sheaf of corn and a little house for the birds. And they'll have mistletoe over the door as well, no doubt. But you wait till I get home; I'll show them!'

At the market there were crowds of people, both big and small, everyone shopping, and there was plenty to choose from! At one stall stood a farmer selling beautiful golden sheaves of corn. As her husband walked past the stall Mrs Pepperpot climbed out from the knapsack pocket and disappeared inside the biggest sheaf of all.

'Hullo, Mr Pepperpot,' said the farmer, 'how about some corn for the birds this Christmas?'

'Too dear!' answered Mr Pepperpot gruffly.

'Oh no, it's not!' squeaked the little voice of Mrs Pepperpot.

'If you don't buy this sheaf of corn I'll tell everyone you're married to the woman who shrinks!'

Now Mr Pepperpot above all hates people to know about his wife turning small, so when he saw her waving to him from the biggest sheaf he said to the farmer: 'I've changed my mind; I'll have that one, please!'

But the farmer told him he would have to wait in the queue.

Only a little girl saw Mrs Pepperpot slip out of the corn and dash into a bird house on Mr Andersen's stall. He was a carpenter and made all his bird houses look just like real little houses with doors and windows for the birds to fly in and out. Of course Mrs Pepperpot chose the prettiest house; it even had curtains in the windows and from behind these she watched her husband buy the very best sheaf of corn and stuff it in his knapsack.

He thought his wife was safe inside and was just about to get on his kick-sledge and head for home, when he heard a little voice calling from the next stall.

'Hullo, Husband!' squeaked Mrs Pepperpot. 'Haven't you forgotten something? You were going to buy me a bird house!'

Mr Pepperpot hurried over to the stall. He pointed to the house with the curtains and said: 'I want to buy that one, please!'

Mr Andersen was busy with his customers. 'You'll have to take your turn,' he said.

So once more poor Mr Pepperpot had to stand patiently in a queue. He hoped that no one else would buy the house with his wife inside.

But she wasn't inside; she had run out of the back door, and now she was on her way to the next stall. Here there was a pretty young lady selling holly and mistletoe. Mrs Pepperpot had to climb up the post to reach the nicest wreath, and there she stayed hidden.

Soon Mr Pepperpot came by, carrying both the sheaf of corn and the little bird house.

The young lady gave him a dazzling smile and said: 'Oh, Mr Pepperpot, wouldn't you like to buy a wreath of mistletoe for your wife?'

'No thanks,' said Mr Pepperpot, 'I'm in a hurry.'

'Swing high! Swing low! I'm in the mistletoe!' sang Mrs Pepperpot from her lofty perch.

When Mr Pepperpot caught sight of her his mouth fell open: 'Oh dear!' he groaned. 'This is too bad!'

With a shaking hand he paid the young lady the right money and lifted the wreath down himself, taking care that Mrs Pepperpot didn't slip out of his fingers. This time there would be no escape; he would take his wife straight home, whether she liked it or not. But just as he was leaving, the young lady said: 'Oh, sir, you're our one hundredth customer, so you get a free balloon!' and she handed him a red balloon.

Before anyone could say 'Jack Robinson' Mrs Pepperpot had grabbed the string and, while Mr Pepperpot was struggling with his purse, gloves and parcels, his tiny wife was soaring up into the sky. Up she went over the marketplace, and soon she was fluttering over the trees of the forest, followed by a crowd of crows and magpies and small birds of every sort.

'Here I come!' she shouted in bird language. For, when Mrs Pepperpot was small, she could talk with animals and birds.

A big crow cawed: 'Are you going to the moon with that balloon?'

'Not quite, I hope!' said Mrs Pepperpot, and she told them the whole story. The birds all squawked with glee when they heard about the corn and the bird house she had got for them.

'But first you must help me,' said Mrs Pepperpot. 'I want you all to hang on to this balloon string and guide me back to land on my own doorstep.'

So the birds clung to the string with their beaks and claws and, as they flew down to

Mrs Pepperpot's house, the balloon looked like a kite with fancy bows tied to its tail.

When Mrs Pepperpot set foot on the ground she instantly grew to her normal size.

So she waved goodbye to the birds and went indoors to wait for Mr Pepperpot.

It was late in the evening before Mr Pepperpot came home, tired and miserable after searching everywhere for his lost wife. He put his knapsack down in the hall and carried the sheaf of corn and the bird house outside. But when he came in again he noticed that the mistletoe had disappeared.

'Oh well,' he said sadly, 'what does it matter now that Mrs Pepperpot is gone?'

He opened the door into the kitchen; there was the mistletoe hanging over the doorway and, under it, as large as life, stood Mrs Pepperpot!

'Darling husband!' she said, as she put her arms round his neck and gave him a great big smacking kiss: 'Happy Christmas!'

# Mrs Pepperpot in the
# Magic Wood

MRS PEPPERPOT, as you may remember, lives on a hillside in Norway. Behind her house there is an old fence with a gate in it. If you walk through that gate, says Mrs Pepperpot, you walk straight into the Magic Wood.

It's really just a little copse with larch and spruce and birch trees, but in spring the ground is covered with snowdrops – the whitest carpet you ever saw, and round a big mossy stone a patch of violets make a bright splash of colour. The birch trees seem more silvery in here and the pale green branches of the larch trees more feathery as they sway over the stream that trickles down the hillside. And in and out of the long grass the weasel has made a pattern of little winding paths. It is very beautiful.

But Mrs Pepperpot likes it even better in winter when the Magic Wood has a thick carpet of snow and the icicles sparkle from the branches. Then all is silent except for the *scrunch, scrunch* of Mrs Pepperpot's boots as she walks through the snow.

It was a day before Christmas, and Mrs Pepperpot had asked her husband to cut her a small Christmas tree in the Magic Wood. But he was so busy at his work that he hadn't had time to do it, so Mrs Pepperpot decided to take the axe and cut it down herself. As the snow was slippery, she took a stick with her. She soon reached the little fir tree and, after marking a circle round it with her stick, she lifted the axe to start chopping.

Then the awful thing happened! You know, the thing that keeps happening to Mrs Pepperpot at the most inconvenient moments: she shrank to the size of a pepperpot.

'I'll have to find a small stick,' she said, 'it'll help me to plough a path through the snow. Ah well, I could be in a worse fix, I suppose, and I ought to be used to it by now.'

'Hi!' shouted a small voice quite close above her.

'What was that?' said Mrs Pepperpot, who had nearly jumped out of her skin, she was so surprised.

'It's me!' said the little voice. And now Mrs Pepperpot could see a tiny boy no bigger than herself, standing by her side.

'Well, come on; don't just stand there! They're all sitting inside, crying their hearts out because they think the ogre has eaten you. We must hurry home and surprise them.'

Without waiting for an answer, the little fellow bent down to a hole in the snow and started to crawl into it.

'Well,' thought Mrs Pepperpot, 'I may as well go and see what this is all about; he seems to know me, even if I don't know him.'

She left the axe and tucking the stick she had found under her arm she bravely crawled after the boy into the hole. It was quite a long tunnel which led to a little door. The boy knocked, but from behind the door there was such a noise of wailing and weeping that at first no one answered his knock. But when he had knocked again the bolt slid back and the door was opened by a young girl

with a ladle in her hand. The room was brightly lit by a fire over which hung a steaming pot. Mrs Pepperpot, who was hidden behind the boy in the dark tunnel, could see three people inside and they were all looking most dejected as they went on with their crying.

The little boy stamped his foot. 'Stop that noise!' he shouted. 'Can't you see I've brought Betty Bodkin back?' and with that he took hold of Mrs Pepperpot's arm and dragged her into the middle of the room.

For a moment everyone stared at Mrs Pepperpot and then the wailing began afresh!

'Little Dick, what have you done? This isn't Betty Bodkin!' said the girl with the ladle.

Little Dick turned and had a good look at Mrs Pepperpot. Then he shook his fists at her and threw himself on the floor in what can only be described as a temper tantrum.

But Mrs Pepperpot had had enough of this nonsense: 'When you've all finished your cater-wauling,' she said, 'perhaps someone will tell me who you are and who I'm *supposed* to be. Then maybe I'll tell you who I *really* am.'

'It is a bit confusing,' said a fat little man who sat nearest the fire, 'we thought you were one of us, you see.'

'So I hear, but who are *you*?' Mrs Pepperpot was losing patience.

'Let me explain,' said the girl with the ladle, and as no one tried to stop her, she continued: 'You may not recognize us, but when you were little you knew us well enough. D'you remember your mother taking you on her lap sometimes to cut your nails? You probably didn't like it, and she would hold your hand and count your fingers one by one.'

'That's right,' said Mrs Pepperpot, 'and then she would sing me a little ditty that went like this:

> *'Here is Thumbkin, fat and tubby,*
> *Here is Lickpot, always grubby,*
> *Longman next: he has his fiddle,*
> *Now Betty Bodkin with her needle,*
> *And little Dick who's just a tiddle.'*

They all clapped their hands. 'There you are!' cried the girl, 'you haven't forgotten. And that's who we are – the finger people who live in the Magic Wood. This is Thumbkin,' she said, pointing to the fat little man by the fire.

'Pleased to meet you,' said Thumbkin, as Mrs Pepperpot shook hands with him.

'I used to find you a very comforting person,' said Mrs Pepperpot smiling.

'This is Longman, as you can see,' went on the girl, but the tall, thin fellow was so shy he held his fiddle behind his back and looked as if he'd like to vanish right away.

'I'm Lickpot. I do the cooking, you see,' said the girl.

Little Dick had now got over his disappointment. Taking another look at Mrs Pepperpot he said: 'You're so very like Betty Bodkin!'

'Just what happened to Betty Bodkin?' asked Mrs Pepperpot.

Immediately they all started talking at once: 'It was like this – we were out in the wood – we always wish the moon a Happy Christmas – it was such a glorious night!'

'One at a time, please!' said Mrs Pepperpot, holding her ears.

Lickpot raised her ladle to get order. 'Quiet now! I'll explain. As they said, we went for a walk to greet the moon. Suddenly a huge ogre came along the path and we all had to rush into the tunnel to get out of his way. But Betty Bodkin tripped over her needle, and didn't manage it. The ogre picked her up in his great hand and put her in his pocket. Now we're all so worried about what has happened to her, and Christmas won't be Christmas without Betty Bodkin!'

'Perhaps the ogre has eaten her up!' said Little Dick, and he started to cry again.

'Oh, ogres aren't as bad as they once were!' said Mrs Pepperpot to comfort him. 'Besides, if she's as used to being small as I am, she'll know how to get out of tight corners.'

'If only we could find where the ogre lives, then perhaps we could rescue her,' said Lickpot.

'I'm sure we could, if we all pull together,' said Mrs Pepperpot. 'I think I have an idea where that ogre lives.'

'Will you show us the way?' asked Little Dick excitedly, and they all crowded round Mrs Pepperpot, tugging at her skirt.

'There's no time to lose,' she said immediately and started crawling back through the tunnel. The others followed, but when they got outside they found the road blocked by an enormous snowdrift.

'We'll never get through that!' said Thumbkin and looked quite ready to creep back to his warm fire inside.

It was quite a problem, and Mrs Pepperpot shut her eyes so as to think better. Suddenly she remembered something very important; they were in the Magic Wood, where wishes come true if you wish hard enough. 'Quiet, everybody! I'm going to make a wish!' she said.

While they all stood very still she touched the snowdrift with her stick and said loudly: 'I wish this snowdrift to turn into a polar bear – a *friendly* polar bear – who can carry us all on his back and take us to the ogre's house.'

As soon as she finished speaking the snowdrift began to rise under them and they found themselves sitting on a soft, warm, white rug. Then the rug began to move forward, and Mrs Pepperpot could see two ears in front of her. She had ridden on a bear before, so she knew what bears like most – to be tickled between the ears. Gingerly she crawled towards the ears and perched herself between them.

'Do be careful!' warned Lickpot, who was clinging with all her might to the bear's fur. Longman was so frightened he was lying full length with his face buried, but Thumbkin and Little Dick were beginning to enjoy themselves, looking all around from their high seat.

When the bear felt his ears being tickled he purred – or rather, he rumbled – with contentment, and in no time at all he had carried Mrs Pepperpot and the finger people to the edge of the wood where there was a fence and a gate in it.

'Open the gate with your muzzle!' commanded Mrs Pepperpot, and the big polar bear did just as she said and opened the gate.

Then they came to a house with a lighted window.

'Now I want you to lie down outside the door,' said Mrs Pepperpot, 'and you must wait there till I come out again – is that clear?'

The great creature just nodded his head slowly and settled down on the doorstep.

Mrs Pepperpot turned to the finger people: 'I'm pretty certain that I'll find the ogre inside this house,' she said.

'Don't you want us to help you rescue Betty Bodkin?' asked Little Dick, who was feeling quite chirpy now.

'No thanks, I think I can manage this by myself,' said Mrs Pepperpot. 'I just want you to wait here with Mr Polar Bear. If Betty Bodkin is there I'll bring her out to you, and then you can all go home.'

They all shook her hand warmly and wished her luck.

'Trust in me!' said Mrs Pepperpot, and swung her leg over the door sill.

Just as she disappeared into the dark hall she grew to her normal size and walked into the dining room.

There sat Mr Pepperpot; the tears were rolling down his cheeks and his sharp nose was quite red with crying. On the table by his side stood a small doll's bed Mrs Pepperpot had bought to give a little girl for Christmas, and in the bed lay Betty Bodkin, trying very hard to look like a doll! There were medicine bottles on the table as well, and a box of liquorice pills.

Mrs Pepperpot put her hands on her hips and said: 'Just what are you carrying on like this for?'

At the sound of her voice Mr Pepperpot looked up. He couldn't believe his eyes!

'Is that you? Is that really you, my own wife?' he cried, and caught hold of her skirt to see if she wasn't a ghost.

'I thought I'd lost you this time! I was going through the wood, searching for you, when I saw . . .' He stopped and stared at the little old woman in the doll's bed. 'But then, who's this? I picked her up in the snow and brought her home, thinking it was you who had shrunk again.'

'You silly man! Mixing me up with a doll that someone has dropped on the path!' said Mrs Pepperpot. Then, standing between him and the doll's bed, she carefully lifted Betty Bodkin up and wiped away the sticky medicine and liquorice pills her husband had tried to dose her with. Betty was just about to thank her, but Mrs Pepperpot made a sign for her to keep quiet and carried her towards the front door.

But Mr Pepperpot was so afraid his wife might vanish once more that he followed, holding on to her coat. As she leaned out of the door he asked: 'What are you putting the doll in that snowdrift for?'

'To get her back where she belongs,' said Mrs Pepperpot. 'Come and have your supper now.'

'Just a minute. I want to shovel that snowdrift away from the doorstep first,' Mr Pepperpot said.

'Why? Are you afraid it'll walk in? Come on now, supper's ready.'

So Mr Pepperpot went into the kitchen to wash his hands and didn't hear his wife whisper to the snowdrift: 'Turn about, quick march and get them home as fast as you can!'

Later that night, when she was washing up, Mrs Pepperpot amused herself by singing the old ditty:

> *'Here is Thumbkin, fat and tubby,*
> *Here is Lickpot, always grubby,*
> *Longman next: he has his fiddle,*
> *Now Betty Bodkin with her needle,*
> *And Little Dick who's just a tiddle.'*

# Mrs Pepperpot and the
# Puppet Show

IT WAS a lovely summer's day, just the day for
an outing. The village sewing club had been
invited to a television show in the nearest town
and they were going by special coach.

Mrs Pepperpot was going too, and very excited
she was, as she had never watched a TV show in
a theatre before. Nor had any of the others, for
that matter, and they had all put on their best
summer frocks and straw hats with flowers.

On the way they prattled, as women do, and
wondered what it would be like. They were going to
see a puppet show, and Sarah South was sure that
everyone else in the village would be envying them.

When they got to the town the bus stopped in the market square and they all got off. As they walked into the hall Norah North said: 'One thing we shouldn't do – smile at the camera – it looks so silly when you're watching TV.'

'Especially if you have gaps in your teeth,' said Mrs East, who could be a bit sharp when she liked.

They felt rather shy when they were given the front row of seats, but soon they were all comfortably seated with little bags of peppermints to munch. All except Mrs Pepperpot. Where was she?

Well, you know how she likes to poke her nose into things, and as they were walking along the passage to their seats, Mrs Pepperpot heard someone sniffing and crying in a little room next to the stage.

'That's funny!' she thought and peeped through the door. There she saw a full-grown man with a top hat and long moustachios, sitting on a chair, crying like a baby.

'Well, I never!' said Mrs Pepperpot, but before she had time to follow the rest of her party, she SHRANK!

As she stood there, a tiny figure by the door in her bright summer dress and little straw hat, the puppet man saw her at once. Quick as a knife he stretched out his hand and picked her up.

'*There* you are!' he said, holding her tightly between finger and thumb. 'I thought I'd lost you!'

Mrs Pepperpot was so terrified she didn't move, but when the man had had a closer look he said: 'But you're *not* my Sleeping Beauty puppet at all!'

'Of course I'm not!' said Mrs Pepperpot. 'The very idea!'

'All the same,' said the puppet man, 'as I can't find my most important puppet, you'll have to play her part. You'll look fine with a blonde wig and a crown and a veil, and I'll make your face up so that you'll be really beautiful.'

'You let me go this minute!' shouted Mrs Pepperpot, struggling to get out of the man's grip. 'Whoever heard of an old woman like me playing Sleeping Beauty?'

'Now, now! You have talent – you can act, I'm sure of it. And that's more than can be said of my other puppets who have to be handled with sticks and threads. You can walk and talk by yourself; you're just what I've always dreamed of and you'll bring me success and lots of money, you'll see.'

'Over my dead body!' said Mrs Pepperpot, who was still furious. 'I don't even remember the story of Sleeping Beauty.'

'I shall be telling the story,' explained the puppet man, 'and you just have to do the things I say. But you don't come into the first act at all, so you can stand at the side and watch the other puppets through that crack in the curtain. Now it's time for the show to start, so be a sport and stay there, won't you?'

'I may and I mayn't,' said Mrs Pepperpot, so he lifted her gingerly down on the side of the puppet stage which was set up in the middle of the real theatre stage.

Then the lights in the hall went out and those on the little stage went on. Mrs Pepperpot peeped through the hole in the curtain. The scene was a magnificent marble hall and she could see a puppet king and queen sitting on their thrones with their courtiers standing round. They were looking at a baby doll in a cradle.

The man began to speak behind the stage.

'There was once a king and a queen who had been blessed with a baby princess.'

'Lucky he didn't want me to lie in the cradle!' thought Mrs Pepperpot.

The man read on, telling how the good fairies were asked to the christening party and how they each gave the little princess a gift. Waving their wands over her cradle the fairies came in one by one.

'May you have the gift of Beauty!' said one.

'May you have the gift of Patience!' said another.

'I could certainly do with that gift,' said Mrs Pepperpot to herself. 'If there's anything I lack it's patience!'

When all the good fairies except one had waved their wands over the cradle, there was a terrible clap of thunder and the stage went completely dark for a moment.

'Goodness Gracious!' cried Mrs Pepperpot, 'I hope they haven't had a breakdown!' She was beginning to get excited about the play now.

The lights came on again, and there was the bad fairy leaning over the baby with her wand.

'Ha, ha!' said the puppet man in an old witch sort of voice. 'Today you are all happy, but this is *my* gift to the princess; in your fifteenth year may you prick your finger on a spindle and die!' And with that the bad fairy vanished in another clap of thunder and blackout.

'Well, if I'm the Sleeping Beauty, I'm a good deal more than fifteen years old and I'm still hale and hearty!' thought Mrs Pepperpot.

The puppet man had now brought on another fairy to tell the king and queen that their daughter would not really die, but only go into a long, long sleep.

'One day a prince will come and wake her up,' said the fairy and that was the end of the first act.

The puppet man was glad to see Mrs Pepperpot still standing there, but he didn't take any chances and caught her up roughly before she could protest. No matter how much she wriggled, she was dressed in the princess's blonde wig with a crown on top and a veil down her back. The worst part was when the puppet man made up her face: ough! It tasted like candle grease!

But when at last he put her down in front of a little mirror, she had to admit she looked rather wonderful.

'Now listen,' said the puppet man. 'I don't mind if you make up your own speeches, but you must follow the story as I tell it, and one thing you must remember; no advertising! It's strictly forbidden on this TV station.'

'Is it indeed!' said Mrs Pepperpot, who had not forgiven him for the rough treatment she had had – why, he'd even pulled her hair! 'We'll see about that!' she muttered.

But there was no time to argue, as the puppet man was preparing to raise the curtain again. The scene was the same as before, but at first it was empty of puppets while the puppet man read the introduction to the next part of the story.

'The king was so anxious to keep his only child safe from all harm that he ordered every spindle in the country to be burned and forbade any more to be made. Meanwhile the princess grew up with all the gifts she had received from the fairies; she was good and beautiful, modest and patient, and everyone loved her. Then one day when she was fifteen years old the king and queen had gone out and she was all alone in the palace. She thought she would explore a bit.'

The puppet man stopped reading and whispered to Mrs Pepperpot: 'This is where you come in! Walk across the marble hall and up the winding staircase in the corner. You'll find the witch at the top, spinning.'

He gave her a little push, and Mrs Pepperpot, in all her princess finery, walked on to the stage as grandly as she could. In the middle of the marble hall she stood still and looked for the staircase. When she saw it she turned to the audience and, pointing to the stairs, she said: 'I have to go up there; I hope it's safe! Always buy planks at Banks, the lumber man!' And up she went, holding her long skirt like a lady.

At the top of the stairs she found the witch puppet sitting, turning her spindle in her hand. 'Why, whatever are you doing with that old-fashioned thing?' asked Mrs Pepperpot.

'I am spinning,' said the puppet man in his old witch voice.

'I call that silly,' said Mrs Pepperpot, 'when you can buy the best knitting wool in town at Lamb's Wool Shop!'

The audience laughed at this, but the puppet man was not amused. However, he couldn't stop now, so he went on with the play, saying in his old witch voice: 'Would you like to spin, my child?'

'I don't mind if I do,' said Mrs Pepperpot. As she took the spindle from the witch's hand, the puppet man whispered to her to pretend to prick herself.

'Ouch!' cried Mrs Pepperpot, sucking her finger and shaking it. 'I need a plaster from Mr Sands, the chemist!'

Again the audience laughed. The puppet man now whispered to her to lie down on the bed to sleep. She asked if he wanted her to snore to make it more lifelike.

'Of course not!' he said angrily, 'and I don't want any advertising for sleeping pills either!'

'Not necessary!' said Mrs Pepperpot, making herself comfortable on the bed. Then she raised her head for a moment and in a sing-song voice she spoke to the people in the audience:

> *'The moment you recline*
> *On a mattress from Irvine*
> *You will fall into a sleep*
> *That is really quite divine!'*

The puppet man had difficulty in getting himself heard through the shouts of laughter that greeted this outrageous poem. But at last he was able to go on with the story – how the princess slept for a hundred years and everyone in the palace slept too. When he got to the bit about the rose hedge growing thicker and thicker round the walls of the palace, Mrs Pepperpot popped her head up again and said:

> *'Quick-growing roses*
> *From Ratlin and Moses.'*

and then pretended to sleep again. She was really getting her revenge on the puppet man, and she was enjoying every minute of it.

The puppet man struggled on, but now the audience laughed at everything that was said, and he began to wonder if he should stop the show. He tried reading again: 'At length the king's son came to the narrow stairs in the tower. When he reached the top he opened the door of the little chamber, and there he saw the most beautiful sight he had even seen – the Sleeping Beauty.'

While the gramophone played soft music to suit the scene, the puppet prince walked up the stairs and came through the door. Mrs Pepperpot winked one eye at the audience and said:

> *'I owe my beautiful skin*
> *To Complexion-Milk by Flyn.'*

The puppet prince walked stiffly over to her bed and stiffly bent down and planted a wooden kiss on her cheek. But this was too much for Mrs Pepperpot: 'No, no!' she shrieked, jumping out of bed and knocking the prince flying, so that all his threads broke and he landed in an untidy heap at the bottom of the stairs.

Down the stairs came Mrs Pepperpot herself, and, jumping over the fallen prince, she rushed across the stage and out through the curtain, while the audience rolled in their seats and clapped and shouted for the princess to come back.

But once safely in the dressing room, Mrs Pepperpot only just had time to snatch off her wig and veil and crown before she grew to her normal

size. The little things she put in her handbag and she walked through the door as calmly as you please, only to be met by the poor puppet man, who was wringing his hands and crying even worse than before the show.

'Whatever's the matter?' asked Mrs Pepperpot.

'My show's ruined!' he wailed. 'They'll never put it on TV again after all that advertising!'

'Advertising!' Mrs Pepperpot pretended to be surprised. 'Wasn't it all part of the play?'

But the puppet man wasn't listening to her: 'Oh dear, oh dear! What will become of me? And now I have no Sleeping Beauty at all!'

'You should treat your puppets with more respect,' said Mrs Pepperpot, 'they don't like being pushed about and having their hair pulled!'

With that she left him and walked out to the square to get on the bus. Her friends had all been too busy laughing and discussing the play to notice that she hadn't been with them. She sat down next to Sarah South who asked her if she had enjoyed the show.

'Oh, I had a lovely time! We all did, I mean!' said Mrs Pepperpot.

A few days later the puppet man was mending the threads of his puppet prince. He was feeling happier now, because all the newspapers had written that his way of playing Sleeping Beauty was new and original, and they all praised his performance very highly.

There was a knock on the door and the postman handed him a small parcel. He wondered what it could be, but when he opened it he stared with astonishment: inside was the princess's wig, crown and veil and also a reel of black thread and a little note. The puppet-man read it aloud:

> *'As back to you these things I send,*
> *May I be bold and recommend*

*When next your puppet prince you mend,*
*Try Jiffy's thread; it will not rend.'*

Who had sent the parcel? And where did that
little puppet go who could walk and talk on its
own?

'If only I knew!' sighed the puppet man.

# Mrs Pepperpot and the
# Baby Crow

ONE SUMMER'S day when Mrs Pepperpot was coming home from picking blueberries in the forest, she suddenly heard something stir in the heather.

'Oh dear,' she thought, 'I hope it isn't a snake.'

She picked up a strong stick and walked as softly as she could towards the noise.

But it wasn't a snake; it was a baby crow which must have fallen out of its nest. It was flapping its wings and trying so hard to get off the ground.

'Poor wee thing!' said Mrs Pepperpot. 'What shall we do with you?'

Very gently she lifted it up and then she could see it had hurt one of its wings. So she put it into her apron pocket and took it home with her. When she got indoors she found a little doll's bed which she lined with soft flannel, and then she carried the baby crow up to the attic, so that Mr Pepperpot wouldn't know about it. He always got so cross when she brought creatures in.

Whenever her husband was out Mrs Pepperpot would sneak up to the attic with little titbits for the bird and watch it hop around on the floor. When it got stronger it could jump from one beam to the other, and soon the day came when it could really fly.

But by now Mrs Pepperpot had got so fond of the untidy ball of black fluff that she hadn't the heart to let it go. The days went by till one Monday morning Mrs Pepperpot woke up and said to herself: 'Today's the day. I'll have to let the bird out today.'

But then the weather turned nasty and she thought it would be better to wait till the next day.

On Tuesday morning the sun shone. In fact, it was very hot.

'Oh dear,' said Mrs Pepperpot, 'I'm sure there'll be a thunderstorm. The poor little thing would be frightened to death. We'd better wait till tomorrow.'

On Wednesday Mrs Pepperpot couldn't find the cat, and she was afraid it might be lurking somewhere outside the house, waiting to pounce on the baby crow. So she decided to wait till Thursday.

On Thursday she found the cat and shut it in the shed. The little crow was flying from beam to beam and quite clearly wanted to get out. When Mrs Pepperpot came up to the attic it flew on to her shoulder and pulled her hair with its beak, as much as to say: 'Come on, open that window!'

But Mrs Pepperpot had thought up another excuse. 'You see, my pet,' she said, stroking the little crow's back, 'when people have been ill, they have to rest a bit – they call it convalescing – before they can go out. I think you need a little more convalescing.'

'Caw, caw!' said the crow and flew off into a corner of the attic where it sulked the rest of the day.

On Friday Mrs Pepperpot spent a lot of time in the attic. She found all sorts of things to do up there, sorting out her boxes of old clothes and quite unnecessarily dusting the shelves. In between she sighed and she sniffed, and by the time her husband came home she was so out of sorts she had forgotten to cook him any supper.

'What's the idea?' said Mr Pepperpot. 'Can't a man even have a meal when he comes back from a hard day's work?'

'Eating! That's all you think of!' snapped Mrs Pepperpot. 'You can come back in half an hour.' And she turned her back on him and made a great noise with the saucepans so that he wouldn't notice she was crying.

'Well!' said Mr Pepperpot, 'I don't know what's the matter with you, but you seem to have lost the *rest* of your wits,' and with that he hurried out of the door, in case his wife should throw a plate after him.

But Mrs Pepperpot was too upset to throw plates; she just stood by the kitchen stove and cried because she couldn't bear to let the little crow fly.

When she went to bed she was feeling more sensible and she told herself she would do it for sure tomorrow. But then she remembered it was Saturday: 'So many people go out shooting on Saturdays, they might shoot my baby by mistake, or think it was lame and "put it out of its misery", as they say.'

So next day she went to the attic, and when the little crow flew over to her, she took it gently in her hand and talked to it soothingly. 'You must be patient a little longer. Today you might get shot, and tomorrow is Sunday and then there are so many trippers about you might get caught and put in a cage. You wouldn't like that, would you, my pet? No, let's wait till the beginning of the week when all is quiet again.'

The bird seemed to understand what she was saying, because it jumped straight out of her hand and flew up and pecked her nose!

'Temper, temper!' said Mrs Pepperpot and she didn't go near the attic the rest of the day.

On the Sunday she only had time to take some food and water up to the bird in the morning, as she was expecting visitors and, besides, Mr Pepperpot was home all day.

On Monday morning she had some nice bacon rind which she took up as a special treat.

'Here we are, my little duck, something really nice for you!' she said.

But the little crow just glared at her from the highest beam and wouldn't come down.

There was a bee buzzing round the window, so, as Mrs Pepperpot was afraid it might sting her precious bird, she opened the window and let it out.

At that very moment she SHRANK!

'Caw, caw! At last!' squawked the little crow, and before she had time to get on her feet, Mrs Pepperpot felt herself being lifted into the air by her skirt, and away went the little crow with her out of the window!

As they flew over the roof and the trees they were joined by a whole crowd of big crows, all squawking together.

'Caw, caw! Welcome back!' they squawked.

One big crow flew up beside the young crow. In a deep throaty voice it said: 'Well done, young 'un. Bring her before the council! We'll all be there. Caw, caw!

'Oh no!' cried Mrs Pepperpot, 'not that again!' Because she remembered the time she had had to sing at the Crows' Festival and they stole all her clothes!

But there was nothing she could do, dangling helplessly, as she was, in the little crow's beak.

All the crows were heading in the same direction and soon they swooped down and landed in a clearing in the forest. The little crow put Mrs Pepperpot down right in the centre, and all the crows stood in a big ring round her. She was very frightened indeed.

The big crow spoke first: 'You may begin, young 'un. Tell us what happened.'

So the little crow told them how Mrs Pepperpot had found it after it had fallen out of the nest, and how she had taken it home.

'Were you frightened!' asked the big crow.

'I suppose I was just as frightened as she is now,' said the little crow, looking at Mrs Pepperpot, who was shaking all over.

'What did the monster do to you?' asked another crow.

'I'm not a monster!' cried Mrs Pepperpot. 'I didn't do anything bad! I just kept him in a nice warm attic till he could fly.'

'That's right,' said the little crow. 'She took pity on me because I had hurt my wing.'

'But after the wing got better,' asked the big crow, 'did she still keep you shut up in the attic against your will?'

'She did,' said the little crow.

'It's a black lie!' shouted Mrs Pepperpot. 'You know I was going to let you out, but I had to be sure you would be safe. The first day you could fly it was raining cats and dogs.'

The big crow looked up at the sky: 'Hm, it looks as if it's going to pour any minute now. We'd better keep the little thing here till tomorrow, or she might get drowned walking home.'

'I'm not a "thing",' said Mrs Pepperpot.

'You called me a "duck",' said the little crow.

'But I *must* get home today,' said Mrs Pepperpot. 'I have to put the peas to soak for our pea soup tomorrow.'

'And we can't let her go tomorrow, either,' went on the big crow, 'because that's the day we have a visit from Master Fox, and he might take her for a weasel.'

'Stuff and nonsense!' said Mrs Pepperpot.

'That's what I thought,' said the little crow, 'when you told me about the cat.'

'Perhaps we could let her go on Wednesday,' chipped in another crow.

'Wednesday!' cried Mrs Pepperpot. 'I must certainly be there then, because that's the day the fishmonger calls, and I've ordered two pounds of herring from him.'

The big crow shook its head: 'I'm afraid that fishmonger's van is too dangerous. It might run her down. She can go on Thursday.'

'Thursday! I *must* be home then; we get the big saw back from the grinder's that day, and I have to help my husband saw up logs.'

'Tut, tut! A little thing like you can't be allowed to saw logs!' said the big crow. He turned to the others: 'Don't you think it would be safer to keep her till Friday?'

'Yes, yes! Caw, caw!' squawked all the crows.

'Friday is my big cleaning day,' said Mrs Pepperpot, 'and if you don't let me go till then I shall have to do all my washing as well. It's not fair!' and she stamped her foot and shook her fists at the birds.

'Now, now,' said the big crow, 'temper, temper! Friday is an unlucky day, everyone says so. Saturday would be better.'

But this was too much for Mrs Pepperpot. She just sat down and buried her head in her apron and sobbed and sobbed. She thought she'd never get home!

'I only did it to be kind!' she hiccoughed. 'I was so very fond of the little crow!'

Just then she felt herself grow to her usual size, and when she looked round all the crows had scattered and were whirling overhead in the trees, cawing loudly.

Mrs Pepperpot wiped her eyes and straightened her hair. Then she started to walk home. As she walked she thought about the things the crows had said to her.

'I think maybe they're right. It isn't much fun to be in prison like that, day after day.'

But wait till you hear the strangest thing: since that day, whenever Mrs Pepperpot goes up to the attic and opens the window, that little crow comes flying in to sit on her shoulder! It never pecks her nose or pulls her hair, and Mrs Pepperpot always has a titbit for it in her apron pocket.

# Mrs Pepperpot Learns to Swim

AS YOU know, Mrs Pepperpot can do almost anything, but, until last summer, there was one thing she couldn't do; she couldn't swim! Now I'll tell you how she learned.

In the warm weather Mrs Pepperpot always took a short cut through the wood when she went shopping. In the middle of the wood is quite a large pool which the village children use. Here they play and splash about in the water. The older ones, who can swim, dive from a rock and race each other up and down the pool. They teach the younger ones to swim too, as there's no grown-up to show them. Luckily, the pool is only deep round the big rock and those who can't swim stay where it's shallow. But they're all very keen to learn, so they practise swimming strokes lying on their tummies over a tree stump, and counting one-two-three-four as they stretch and bend their arms and legs.

Mrs Pepperpot always stopped to watch them, and then she would sigh to herself and think: 'If only I could do that!' Because nobody had taught *her* to swim when she was a little girl.

Some of the big boys could do the crawl, and the little ones tried to copy them, churning up the water with their feet and their arms going like windmills while everyone choked and spluttered.

'I bet I could learn that too!' thought Mrs Pepperpot. 'But where could I practise?'

One day when she got home, she decided to try some swimming strokes in the kitchen, but no sooner had she got herself balanced on her tummy over the kitchen stool, when her neighbour knocked on the door asking to borrow a cup of flour. Another time she tried, she flung out her arms and knocked the saucepan of soup off the stove, and her husband had to have bread and dripping for supper. He was *not* pleased.

Every night she would dream about swimming. One night she had a lovely dream in which she could do the breast stroke most beautifully. As

she dreamed, she stretched forward her arms, bent her knees and then. – Wham! One foot almost kicked a hole in the wall, the other knocked Mr Pepperpot out of bed!

Mr Pepperpot sat up. 'What's the matter with you?' he muttered. 'Having a nightmare, or something?'

'Oh no,' answered Mrs Pepperpot, who was still half in a dream. 'I'm swimming, and it's the most wonderful feeling!'

'Well, it's not wonderful for me, I can tell you!' said Mr Pepperpot crossly. 'You stop dreaming and let me have some peace and quiet.' And he climbed into bed and went to sleep again.

But Mrs Pepperpot couldn't stop dreaming about swimming. Another night she dreamed she was doing the crawl – not like the little ones, all splash and noise, but beautiful strong, steady strokes like the big boys, and one arm went up and swept the flowerpots from the windowsill and the other landed smack on Mr Pepperpot's nose.

This was too much for Mr Pepperpot. He sat up in bed and shook Mrs Pepperpot awake.

'You stop that, d'you hear!' he shouted.

'I was only doing the crawl' said Mrs Pepperpot in a faraway voice.

'I don't care if you were doing a high dive or a somersault!' Mr Pepperpot was very angry now. 'All I know is you need water for swimming and not a bed. If you want to swim go jump in a swimming pool and get yourself a swimming teacher!'

'That's too expensive,' said Mrs Pepperpot, who was now awake. 'I watch the children in the pool in the wood. One of these days, when they're all gone home, I'll have a try myself.'

'Catch your death of cold, no doubt,' muttered Mr Pepperpot and dozed off again. But a little while later there was a terrible crash, and this time Mr Pepperpot nearly jumped out of his skin.

There was Mrs Pepperpot, on the floor, rubbing a large lump on her forehead. She had been trying to dive off the side of the bed!

'You're the silliest woman I ever knew!' said Mr Pepperpot. 'And I've had enough! I'm going to sleep on the kitchen floor.'

With that he gathered up the eiderdown and a pillow, went into the kitchen and slammed the door.

Mrs Pepperpot was a bit puzzled. 'I can't have done it right!' But then she decided enough was

enough and, wrapping herself in the only blanket that was left on the bed, she slept the rest of the night without any more swimming dreams.

Then came a bright warm day when all the village children were going on a picnic up in the mountains.

'That's good,' thought Mrs Pepperpot, 'there'll be no one in the pool today and I can get my chance to have a try.'

So when she'd cleaned the house and fed the cat and the dog, she walked through the wood to the pool.

It certainly looked inviting, with the sun shining down through the leaves and making pretty patterns on the still water. There was no one else about.

She sat down on the soft grass and took off her shoes and stockings. She had brought a towel with her, but she'd never owned a bathing suit, and it didn't even occur to her to take her skirt and blouse off. Peering over the edge, she could see the water wasn't very deep just there, so she stood up and said to herself: 'All right, Mrs P, here goes!' and she jumped in!

But she might have known it – at this moment she SHRANK!

Down, down she went, and now, of course, the pool seemed like an ocean to the tiny Mrs Pepperpot.

'Help, help!' she cried, 'I'm drowning!'

'Hold on!' said a deep throaty voice from below. 'Rescue on the way!' And a large frog swam smoothly towards her.

'Get on my back,' he said.

Mrs Pepperpot was thrashing about with both arms and legs and getting tangled up in her skirt as well, but she managed to scramble on to the frog's knobbly back.

'Thanks!' she panted, as they came to the top, and she spat out a lot of water.

The frog swam quickly to the rock, which now seemed quite a mountain to Mrs Pepperpot, but she found a foothold all right and sat down to get her breath, while the frog hopped up beside her.

'You're certainly a good swimmer,' said Mrs Pepperpot.

The frog puffed himself up importantly: 'I'm the champion swimming teacher in this pool,' he said.

'D'you think you could teach me to swim?' asked Mrs Pepperpot.

'Of course. We'll begin right away, if you like.'

'The children do the breaststroke first, I've noticed,' said Mrs Pepperpot.

'That's right, and frogs are very good at that. You climb on my back and watch what I do,' said the frog, as he jumped in.

It was a bit difficult to get off the rock on to the frog's back, but he trod water skilfully and kept as steady as he could. Soon she was safely perched and watched how the frog moved his arms and legs in rhythm. After a while he found her a little piece of floating wood and told her to hang on to that while she pushed herself along with her legs.

She got on fine with this till she suddenly lost her grip on the piece of wood and found herself swimming along on her own.

'Yippee!' she shouted with excitement, but the frog, who had been swimming close to her all the time, now came up below her and lifted her on to his back.

'That's enough for the moment,' he said, and took her back to the rock for a rest. 'You've got the idea very well, for a beginner.'

Mrs Pepperpot was feeling so pleased with herself, she wanted to go straight on and learn the crawl and swim on her back and everything, but the frog said: 'Not so fast, my dear; you've learned to keep afloat now, but you must go on practising the breaststroke before you can do the other things.' But when he saw she looked disappointed, he said: 'I'll get my tadpoles to give you a show of water acrobatics, how's that? You get in and swim along with me to the shallow end; that's where they have their water circus.'

So they set off together, the frog making elegant circles round Mrs Pepperpot as she made her way slowly across the pool, trying to remember to keep her arms together and her legs from kicking in all directions. At last they got to the shallow part where there were reeds growing on the sandy bottom, and in and out of these hundreds of tadpoles were darting. There were all sizes from the tiniest things no bigger than a ladybird to big ones with their front legs showing and some even had their back legs as well and were just about to shed their tails.

The frog found a small flat rock for Mrs Pepperpot to sit on and then he called all the tadpoles round him: 'Come on, children,' he croaked, 'I want you to show this lady all your best tricks. Let's see what you can do and remember what I've taught you.'

All the tadpoles immediately got into line, the biggest at the front, the smallest at the back, so that they looked like a long, winding snake. Talk of follow-my-leader! Whatever the front tadpole did, the others copied so exactly you would think they had all been tied together with string. First they swam to the top of the water, then they dived to the bottom, then they wove in and out of the reeds in a beautiful pattern. Then, like aeroplanes doing aerobatics, they rolled over and over and looped the loop and they even swam backwards, still keeping as smartly in line as any regiment of soldiers.

Mrs Pepperpot was very impressed, and the frog had puffed himself up so much, he was nearly bursting with pride.

When the show was over Mrs Pepperpot looked at the frog very pleadingly and said: 'Don't you think you could just show me how you dive? I *would* like to try that.'

'Well,' he said, 'you won't find it very easy to begin with, but it would do no harm to try at this end, I suppose. I'll give you a demonstration first.' And with that he made a perfect dive off the little rock.

When he came up again he told Mrs Pepperpot to point her arms straight up and to let herself go forwards till they were pointing down into the water.

'Shut your eyes as you go in,' he warned.

Mrs Pepperpot stood on the edge of the rock.

'It looks a bit deep,' she said. She was feeling rather frightened.

'It has to be,' said the frog, 'or you'd knock your head on the bottom. Off you go now; I'll be here to save you!'

So Mrs Pepperpot pointed her arms in the air, held her breath, shut her eyes and let herself fall forward. But instead of the beautiful dive she had hoped to make right under the water and up again, she found herself rolling about in what seemed more like a large puddle than a deep pool; she had GROWN!

As she picked herself up and waded out of the water to the bank she could see no sign of the frog or the tadpoles. Her clothes were clinging to her, and though she tried to dry her arms and legs, it was no use putting on her shoes and stockings, so she hurried home in her bare feet, leaving a great dripping trail behind her.

As soon as she got home she remembered what her husband had said: 'You'll catch your death of cold!' So she changed into dry clothes and hid the wet ones in the attic. Then she quickly set about making her husband's favourite macaroni pie for supper.

It was several days before Mrs Pepperpot got a chance to go back to the pool. But all the time she was longing to find out if she had really learned to swim. So, when she heard the children going home through the wood one warm evening, she slipped out of the house and made for the pool as fast as she could go. She looked pretty queer, because this time she was wearing an old long bathing suit of her husband's she had found in the attic, and over it she had her winter coat. She just hoped that no one would see her.

When she got to the pool all was quiet. She didn't dare to dive in, but from the big rock she let herself slide into the water, and before she knew it, there she was, swimming along – not quite as stylishly as the frog, rather more like a dog paddling – but still, she was swimming and Mrs Pepperpot felt very proud.

As she turned to swim back to the rock she noticed she was being followed. There was the frog, keeping pace with her, and behind him were all the tadpoles, in close formation, from the largest to the tiniest, no bigger than a lady-bird! For one moment the frog came to the top of the water and gave a loud croak.

'Thanks, Mr Frog,' said Mrs Pepperpot, 'you're the best swimming teacher in the world!'

With an elegant kick of his back legs, the frog did a nosedive down into the dark depths of the pool, and all the tadpoles followed after and Mrs Pepperpot couldn't see them any more.

So now you know how Mrs Pepperpot learned to swim.

# Mrs Pepperpot Gives a Party

MRS PEPPERPOT likes animals, as you know, but until lately Mr Pepperpot wasn't so keen; in fact, he didn't like *baby* animals at all.

'Messy things,' he used to say, 'always getting in the way and making too much noise!'

'It's all very well for you,' said Mrs Pepperpot, 'out seeing people all day long. But I'm here all alone, and I like to have little creatures round me for company.'

There was no answer to that, so Mr Pepperpot would go off to work muttering: 'Just keep them out of my way, that's all!'

One day when a stray kitten came to the door mewing to come in, Mrs Pepperpot picked it up and brought it indoors. Then she found it had lost a bit of its tail, and though it was mending, it was still very sore.

'Oh, you poor stumpy wee thing!' said Mrs Pepperpot, stroking the kitten, which was trembling with cold and hunger. 'I'll put you in the box under the stove where it's nice and warm, and you shall have some bread and milk.'

Soon the kitten was sleeping contentedly in the box and was so quiet that Mr Pepperpot never noticed it was there when he came home from work.

A few days later, when Mrs Pepperpot was bringing her shopping home from the village, she came past Mr Hog's pigsty, where the sow had had twelve piglets. She stopped to watch them scampering round, and then she noticed that one of them was limping. It was the smallest of the litter and all the other piglets were pushing it about, so that it couldn't even get to its mother to suckle.

'You're having a pretty thin time, Squiggly,' said Mrs Pepperpot, as she leaned over the fence and picked up the piglet, which was now squealing loudly. Just then the farmer came out to feed the sow, and Mrs Pepperpot held up the piglet to show him.

'Look, Mr Hog, this piglet has broken its leg!'

'So it has!' said Mr Hog. 'Well, we'll have to have roast suckling pig for dinner this Sunday.'

He reached out to take the animal from her, but Mrs Pepperpot said: 'Oh no, that would be a shame!' and hung on to the piglet which was quietly grunting by now.

'What else can I do? The others will kill it if I leave it in the sty,' said Mr Hog.

'I'll buy it from you and rear it by hand,' said Mrs Pepperpot, though she wondered how she was going to pay for it.

'I'll give it to you and welcome, Mrs Pepperpot, if you think you can do anything with it,' said Mr Hog.

So Mrs Pepperpot thanked him and went home with the piglet in her arms. When she got there she fixed a little wooden splint on the piglet's broken leg, gave him a good feed of milk and gruel and tucked him up in the box under the stove together with the kitten.

When Mr Pepperpot came home he was a bit startled to hear grunts from under the stove, but Mrs Pepperpot quickly explained that the piglet was a present from Mr Hog.

'It won't cost much to rear,' she said, 'we have plenty of potato peelings and scraps, and then when it's big enough we can sell it.'

This idea appealed to Mr Pepperpot, who liked to make a bit of extra money, so he didn't grumble any more.

Stumpy, the kitten, and Squiggly, the piglet, got on very well together, and Mrs Pepperpot had a lot of fun watching them.

'Good things always come in threes,' she said to herself; 'I wonder what my third pet will be?'

She didn't have long to wait, because the next time she was down at the village store there was a man in there with a sack on his back. She could see there was something moving in the sack, so when they got outside she couldn't help asking what it was.

'Oh, it's just a puppy I'm going to drown,' said the man, who had a nasty leer on his face.

'A puppy?' exclaimed Mrs Pepperpot. 'What's the poor little thing done that you have to drown it?'

'He was the ugliest of the litter,' said the man, 'and as he's not pure-bred anyway, nobody wanted him.'

'Not pure-bred, eh?' Mrs Pepperpot was getting angry. 'Ugly, is he? Well, you wouldn't win much of a prize at a beauty show yourself, mister! If you don't want the puppy you can give him to me; I'll see he gets a good home.'

'All right, all right, keep your hair on!' said the man, undoing the sack and lifting out a small black and white puppy with a pug nose and a patch over one eye. 'He's all yours, free and for nothing!'

He handed the puppy to Mrs Pepperpot and walked off quickly before she could change her mind.

Mrs Pepperpot held the whimpering, frightened little puppy and stroked him: 'Well, Ugly, I don't know what Mr Pepperpot's going to say to another baby in the house, but I couldn't let you be drowned, could I?'

When she got home she put him in with the other two, and he wagged his little tail and made friends with the kitten and the piglet with no trouble at all. Mrs Pepperpot decided to tell her husband she was only keeping the puppy till she could find a home for it, but she didn't have to worry, for Mr Pepperpot never noticed the new addition to the family when he got back from work.

He sat down at the table and his eyes had a far-away look as he said: 'D'you know, wife – I've been thinking.'

'What have you been thinking?' asked his wife.

'There's one thing I've never been and I'd really like to be?' said Mr Pepperpot.

'Whatever can that be?' she wondered, thinking of all sorts of things Mr Pepperpot had never been.

'President of a club or society,' he said.

'Well!' said Mrs Pepperpot, she hadn't expected him to say that. 'Which club or society were you thinking of?'

'I don't know, but Eddie East told me the Sports Club is looking for a new president, and old Hatchet, the president of the Savings Club, died just last week, and then there's the Egg Co-operative Society . . .'

Mrs Pepperpot thought a bit, then she said: 'The best thing would be to give a party.'

'How d'you mean, give a party?' said Mr Pepperpot, who never liked to ask people to the house in case Mrs Pepperpot did her shrinking act.

'Oh, I don't mean a *big* party, just to ask the Easts and the Wests – he's secretary in the Savings Club, you know – in for coffee and cakes one evening. Then, let me see, who's in the Egg Co-operative? Oh yes, that's Sarah South's husband, so we'll ask them too. What about next Saturday?'

Mrs Pepperpot was getting quite excited at the idea of giving a party, but her husband looked very doubtful. He shook his head: 'Not unless you promise not to shrink,' he said.

'Don't be silly,' said Mrs Pepperpot, 'you know I can't do that. But I *will* promise to get out of the way if I do shrink.'

'That's all very well,' said Mr Pepperpot, 'but how shall *I* know where you are?'

'When you hear a mouse squeak three times, you'll know it's me,' said Mrs Pepperpot, and when her husband still looked worried, she handed him a big plate of his favourite macaroni pie.

'Don't you fret,' she said, 'it'll be all right. Goodness! I've just remembered; if we ask the Easts and the Wests and the Souths, we shall *have* to ask the Norths as well.'

'Why? Ned North isn't in any society that I know of,' grumbled Mr Pepperpot. He wished now that he had never started the idea.

'All the same, we've been to their house, and this is a good way to ask them back. Let me see, that'll be eight guests: I shall have to make two layer cakes and lots of little sandwiches.'

'One thing I do know,' said Mr Pepperpot, 'all those stray animals of yours will have to go out in the shed that night.'

'Certainly not!' cried his wife. 'They'd catch their death of cold! They're very well-behaved and will stay right where they are – under the kitchen stove!'

So the day was fixed and the guests all said they would come.

Mrs Pepperpot spent the whole day cleaning the house and baking layer cakes and making sandwiches. Then she put on her Sunday best and stood at the door to welcome her guests and everyone shook hands.

'Now do sit down and make yourselves at home,' said Mrs Pepperpot, bustling about. To her husband, who was standing in a corner looking helpless, she said: 'You'll keep everyone happy, won't you dear, while I go out and heat the coffee?' And then she disappeared out into the kitchen.

Poor Mr Pepperpot! He was so unused to company that he didn't know where to begin, but just stood there shuffling his feet and scratching his head until, luckily, Mr East asked him a question.

'Are you going in for the skiing competition this year?' he asked.

'Well, I might,' said Mr Pepperpot, easing himself into a chair next to Mr East. 'I used to be pretty good when I was young, but of course I'm out of training now.'

'Oh, it wouldn't take you long to get back into form!' Mr East assured him and Mr Pepperpot forgot his shyness and was soon talking away about the races he had won and the spills he had had while all the rest of the party listened. It wasn't until he couldn't think of anything more to tell that he noticed his wife hadn't come back from the kitchen.

'Excuse me a moment,' he said, and rushed out, fearing the worst had happened. But there stood Mrs Pepperpot, as large as life, putting the finishing touches to the layer cakes.

'What's the matter?' she asked.

'Thank goodness you're still here!' said Mr Pepperpot.

'Of course I am! Everything's ready now, so hold the door open for me while I carry in the tray.'

They could hear the guests laughing in the living room, and when they went in they found the piglet had sneaked in and was trying to run round the table.

'Did you ever see a sillier-looking piglet with a wooden splint on?' said Mrs Pepperpot, picking him up. 'I call him Squiggly, but my husband is so fond of pigs he wouldn't even let me get rid of the thing.'

Mr Pepperpot was so surprised to hear his wife say this that he took the pig from her and stroked it, muttering, 'Oh yes, I *love* piglets.' Then he handed it to Mrs North who wanted to hold it on her knee.

All went well while they sat at the table; everyone enjoyed the coffee and the delicious sandwiches and layer cakes. As they chatted Mrs Pepperpot cleverly brought the conversation round to savings. She told Mr West: 'My husband is such a good manager; he always knows exactly what money we have to spend on what!' Which was true enough, for he usually just said 'no' whenever she asked for money to spend on anything except food.

Mr West said, 'Is that so?' and started asking Mr Pepperpot some questions. Soon they were talking about all sorts of money matters, so Mr Pepperpot didn't notice his wife leaving the room again. When he looked up and found her gone he quickly excused himself to go and look for her.

She was not in the kitchen!

Frantically he called: 'Wife! Where are your?'

'Here I am!' she answered, as calmly as you please. She had been to the bedroom to fetch a pillow for Mrs East's back.

'Oh dear, I don't know where I am when you keep disappearing like this!' said Mr Pepperpot.

'I wish you'd stop fussing and just look after our guests,' Mrs Pepperpot said.

Just then they heard a great noise of laughter and squeaks and yaps, and when they opened the door to the living room there were Mr North and Mr East on their hands and knees on the floor, while Squiggly the pig and Ugly the pup were chasing each other round and round the two men. Everyone else was laughing and clapping and egging them on.

'You certainly know how to amuse your guests!' said Mr West, who was too fat to join in the fun on the floor.

'My husband just loves to have animals around,' said Mrs Pepperpot. 'I never know what he's

going to bring home next.' She gave her husband a great nudge to make him say something nice, but Mr Pepperpot was so overcome by all the things that were happening he just said, 'Mm, Ah!' and shooed the pup and the piglet back into the kitchen.

Now Mrs Pepperpot thought it was time they talked about hens, as her husband had said that he might like to be president of the Egg Co-operative Society. So she told the guests how well he looked after their hens and what wonderful eggs they produced. She even told them how he always knew what to do if one of the hens became ill.

Her husband listened in astonishment as he knew very well that it was Mrs Pepperpot who looked after the hens and he hardly ever saw them, but he couldn't stop her now, so he just let her talk till the guests got up and said it was time to go home.

'We've had such a nice evening,' said Norah North as they shook hands at the door, and all the others said much the same, while Mr Pepperpot held a torch for them to see their way down the path.

After they were all safely away he came indoors. Taking out his spotted handkerchief, he wiped his face and said: 'Am I glad that's over! All the same I don't really think they'll make me president of any of their societies.'

A squeaky little voice answered: 'You wait and see!'

Startled, Mr Pepperpot looked round: 'Who said that?' he asked.

'Peep, peep, peep!' said the little voice, and then he remembered that this was the signal his wife was to give him if she had turned small.

'Where are you hiding now?' he asked, but she wanted to tease him, so she let him search all through the house before she told him.

'Here I am!' she called at last from a drawer under the kitchen stove. 'I've decided to sleep with *your* pets tonight!'

'*My* pets!' he snorted, 'what's come over you? I never heard you tell so many fibs in all the years we've been married.'

'I was only trying to help,' said Mrs Pepperpot in her tiny voice, 'and, as a matter of fact, I think I managed it rather well! As they were going down the path I heard Ned North say to his wife that he thought you'd be the right person to be president of the Society for the Protection of Helpless Animals.'

'Well, I'll be blowed!' said Mr Pepperpot.

'I hope you're pleased,' said Mrs Pepperpot. 'I did my best. And now I think I'll say goodnight!' and she snuggled down with Stumpy, the kitten, Squiggly, the piglet and Ugly, the pup.

As for Mr Pepperpot, well, he'd got his wish, they really did ask him to be president of the Society for the Protection of Helpless Animals, and from then on he had to be kind to *all* animals, whether he liked them or not.

# Mrs Pepperpot's Outing

## I

IT WAS a beautiful sunny summer morning, and Mrs Pepperpot was standing at her kitchen window peeling onions. You remember Mrs Pepperpot? She's the little old woman who lives on a hillside in Norway and has the habit of shrinking to the size of a pepperpot at the most inconvenient moments.

Well, here she was, peeling onions, and from time to time she sniffed a little, the way people do when they are peeling onions. As the tears rolled down her cheeks she wiped them away with the back of her hand and sighed. She was not feeling very happy.

But Mr Pepperpot was; he was on holiday. Now he came rushing through the door with his hat askew, and his hair all over the place. Waving his arms, he shouted: 'I've good news for you, Mrs P! Guess what it is.'

'Good news?' said Mrs Pepperpot. 'Have you found me a new pet?' Because she had just been thinking how empty and sad the house was without even a cat or a dog.

'No, no, something *much* better. You'll have to have another guess,' said her husband. 'Pets! How can you be so old-fashioned? They're a dead loss when you want to go away anywhere, always needing to be fed and looked after.'

'But I *like* looking after animals; they're fun,' she answered. 'Besides, quite often one doesn't really *want* to go away, and then it's very useful to be able to say you have to look after the animals.' She wiped away another tear: 'Oh, these onions!'

'Well, I think you're behind the times,' said Mr Pepperpot. 'It's good for everyone to get about and not be stuck in one place all your life.'

This made Mrs Pepperpot laugh. 'Did you say get about? How far do we get in your old wreck of a car? The person who's stuck in one place is *you* with your head under the bonnet every night for weeks on end!'

'It's my hobby,' said Mr Pepperpot. 'Everyone should have a hobby nowadays. It says in the paper you should make good use of your free time.'

You see, Mr Pepperpot had bought an old car cheaply, and ever since he had been tinkering with it, putting in new parts and cleaning and polishing it.

'You still haven't guessed my news, so I'll tell you,' he said. 'We're going for an outing in the car!'

'You mean you've really got it working?' Mrs Pepperpot could hardly believe it. 'Where are we going?'

'There's a car rally over the other side of Blocksberg: it's for old cars, so I thought I might enter mine. I might even win a cup.'

This was a sore point with Mr Pepperpot. His wife knew he had always wanted to win a cup or a trophy. They did have one in the house, but she kept it hidden at the back of a cupboard, because it was one *she* had won when she was a young girl, and worked on a farm. She had got it for being so good at looking after the livestock. Now she would really like Mr Pepperpot to have one too, so she said:

'Yes, let's go. An outing would be fun, and we can take a picnic.'

'I'll just go and check the engine once more; be ready in half an hour.'

Mrs Pepperpot bustled about; she was quite looking forward to seeing some new places after the long winter at home. She got out the picnic basket, hard-boiled some eggs, packed bread and butter and a piece of cold ham and some pancakes left over from last night. As she worked she made up a little song to sing in the car. This is how it went, to the tune of 'Nuts in May':

'My hubby is mad about motoring,
Motoring, motoring,
He spends his evenings tinkering
On his rickety automobile.

So now we'll be bouncing up and down
Up and down, up and down,
Everything in the back seat is thrown
Off the rickety automobile!

I may be crazy to go with him,
Go with him, go with him,
But oh, he's made it look so trim,
His rickety automobile!

*At least we'll have a fine picnic,*
*A fine picnic, a fine picnic,*
*With sausages, bread and ham and chick*
*In his rickety automobile!*

*And then of course we'll see the sights,*
*See the sights, see the sights,*
*Of valleys and forests and mountain heights*
*From his rickety automobile!*

*Hooray!'*

Mr Pepperpot grumbled when she brought the loaded basket out to the car. 'What do we want with all that stuff? Much better to buy ice cream as we go along and there are plenty of cafes where we can have a hot dog and ketchup.' He liked to show that he knew what tourists did when they went motoring.

'No nourishment in ice cream,' said Mrs Pepperpot. 'And I don't trust cafes.' With that she dumped the basket on the back seat and got in.

Mr Pepperpot got in the driving seat. But just before he started the engine he had a sudden thought: 'You won't *shrink* while we're out, will you?'

'Oh, stop fussing!' said Mrs Pepperpot, as she settled herself comfortably. 'You know I never have any idea when it's going to happen. If it does, it does, and I usually manage, don't I? Start up, Mr P, I'm quite looking forward to this outing!'

So off they went. At first Mr Pepperpot drove very carefully down the little country road from the house. But once they were on the main road, with its smooth asphalt surface, he put his foot on the pedal and they hummed along at quite a good pace. He started to whistle; Mr Pepperpot always did that when he was happy.

'This is the life!' he sang. 'All these years I've been mucking about with an old horse and cart, never getting anywhere, never seeing anything.'

'I don't know,' said Mrs Pepperpot. 'You used to get around quite well on a bicycle – fast enough to break your neck!'

'Yes, but think of the advantages of a motor car: four wheels, comfortable seats, plenty of room for luggage and a roof to keep the rain out.'

'Plenty of expense too,' answered Mrs Pepperpot, 'and plenty of time needed for repairs. When will you ever get around to clearing the drains or help me dig up potatoes now?'

'Stop grumbling and enjoy yourself!' ordered Mr Pepperpot as he slowed down over a little bridge. On the other side there was a kiosk selling ice cream.

'There, didn't I tell you we could get ice cream!' said Mr Pepperpot. 'I'll go and get you one.' So he hopped out of the car and went over to the kiosk to buy a double vanilla cornet for Mrs Pepperpot. 'That should put her in a good mood,' he said to himself, as he balanced his way back towards the car with it. But halfway there he was distracted by a hissing noise in the grass at his feet.

'Oops!' he said, and dropped the beautiful ice-cream!

There was nothing for it but to go back for another. He paid his money and the girl gave him a second ice cream as big as the first. Back he went, holding the cornet with its great mound on top very steady. But as he passed the place where he had spilt the first one, he made the mistake of looking down. And do you know? The ice cream

on the ground was *moving*! Poor Mr Pepperpot
dropped the second cornet on the first one and
fled back to the kiosk. He was sure there was a
snake in the grass, and he was very much afraid
of snakes.

But back at the kiosk a busload of trippers had
just lined up for refreshments and Mr Pepperpot
had to stand at the end of the queue.

And what was going on down there in the
grass where two double ice creams were bubbling
and churning like porridge on the boil? You've
guessed it: Mrs Pepperpot was underneath! She
had got out of the car to stretch her legs, and then,

suddenly, she had SHRUNK to the size of a pepperpot!

There she was, right in Mr Pepperpot's path; she was so afraid he might step on her that she hissed like a snake, and the next thing she knew, she was struggling to get her head clear of a freezing cold and sticky mess! She had only just started breathing again when dollop! She was covered with another portion of ice cream as big, cold and sticky as the first!

Poor Mrs Pepperpot didn't know what to do; she'd never be able to dig her way out alone. 'I'll just freeze to death,' she thought miserably. But after a little while she felt the load of ice cream growing lighter, and soon she could push her head through.

'That's better!' she said.

'It's jolly good!' said a voice next to her, and there stood a young kitten, licking his chops and purring.

'What a beautiful, clever little pussy you are!' cried Mrs Pepperpot, wiping the ice cream from her face.

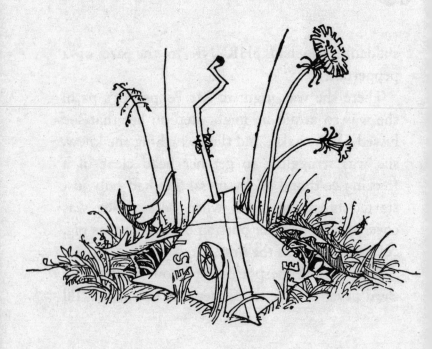

'Mm, can't say *you're* exactly beautiful, but you taste very good,' said the kitten. 'Are you made of ice cream right through? I mean, will I be able to eat you all up?'

'Certainly not!' cried Mrs Pepperpot. 'Ice cream right through indeed! What an idea! No, my friend, I'm just an ordinary woman most of the time. But now and then I shrink to this size. Come to think of it, I don't mind if you do lick me clean – help yourself!'

The kitten set to work very willingly. He was so thorough that soon Mrs Pepperpot had to shout to him to stop.

'I'm very ticklish, you see,' she said, laughing. 'Fancy me getting a catlick; I never expected *that* when we set off in the car this morning.'

'You have a car?' asked the kitten.

'My husband does; we're on an outing – or we were till this happened. Where do you live?'

The kitten hung his head: 'Nowhere, really. I did live in a barn with my mother, but some people came along and picked me up. They took me back to their house and gave me lots of food – that's where I got my taste for ice cream. They used to play with me and at night they would tuck me up in a little basket. It was a wonderful life!'

'What happened then?

'Well, they didn't belong in this place – they were just on holiday. So suddenly, yesterday, they packed up all their stuff, locked the door of the house and got in their car and drove off. I thought I was going too, of course, but they must have forgotten all about me, because they didn't even bother to look back or wave goodbye.'

'I see,' said Mrs Pepperpot, looking thoughtful. 'So now you have no home?'

'No,' said the kitten, 'there's no one to feed me or play with me or call me in at night. Until I found you and the ice cream I hadn't had anything to eat since yesterday.' He licked the last bit of ice-cream out of Mrs Pepperpot's ear with the point of his rough tongue.

'It was just as well I did shrink today,' said Mrs Pepperpot. 'People like that shouldn't be allowed to keep pets. 'Animals are not just playthings for children to throw away when they don't need them any more. Fancy going off and not even asking a

neighbour to look after you!' Mrs Pepperpot was getting really worked up, as she always did when people were thoughtless or unkind to animals.

The kitten was watching her with his head on one side: 'Couldn't you take me home with you and let me be your pussy? You're fond of animals, aren't you? And you can talk cat language.'

'Well,' said Mrs Pepperpot, 'there are one or two snags. My husband is *not* very fond of animals, especially young kittens. And as to understanding cat language, I can only do that when I am small.'

'Will you grow large again soon?'

'I don't know.'

'Will I be afraid of you when you do?'

Mrs Pepperpot laughed. 'I shouldn't think so. But if you could manage to carry me on your back over to that old car there, I might grow to my normal size quite soon.'

'I'll try. Climb up!'

But though Mrs Pepperpot got on his back all right, she was too heavy for the kitten to carry.

'Perhaps I could pull you along by your skirt,' he suggested.

'I don't mind what you do,' said Mrs Pepperpot, as she lay down on the ground with her arms tucked under her head; 'pull away!'

The kitten took Mrs Pepperpot's skirt between his teeth and dragged her as carefully as he could down the path, trying to avoid the ice cream puddle and empty cartons and drinking straws that people had dropped.

'I hope I'm not bumping you too much,' said the kitten.

'Not at all,' answered Mrs Pepperpot, 'I have a fine view of the sky overhead and the birds and the trees.'

But now we had better see what was happening to Mr Pepperpot. We left him in the queue and he stood there a long, long time before he got served again. This time he bought the biggest possible cornet and made straight for the car, hoping Mrs Pepperpot had not lost patience with him altogether.

'Supposing she has shrunk and I won't be able to find her?' he thought anxiously, but when he opened the back door of the car, there she sat, as large as life.

'Oh my! Am I glad to see you!' He sighed with relief.

'You sound as if I'd been to the moon and back,' she said.

'Well, you see, if you had shrunk and disappeared, I'd never have got through all this ice cream.' And he held out the cornet.

'Get along with you – I told you to stop fussing,' said Mrs Pepperpot. She set the cornet carefully into the corner of the basket.

'Aren't you going to eat it after all that?' Mr Pepperpot sounded a little hurt.

'All in good time. We'd better be getting on now, if you're going to enter for the rally.'

'I'm not sure I'll bother with that car rally,' he said. 'While I was standing in the queue at the kiosk I heard someone talking about a cross-country race, and it's not as far to drive as the car rally. Shall we go there instead?'

'It's all one to me,' said Mrs Pepperpot, 'as long as we're enjoying ourselves.'

Mr Pepperpot beamed. 'Yes, we are, aren't we?'

He didn't know that Mrs Pepperpot meant herself and the kitten, which was safely hidden in the basket and enjoying a good lick at that giant ice cream.

## II

The road was smooth and they were driving along quite comfortably when Mr Pepperpot suddenly stopped the car.

'Did you hear something?' he asked his wife.

She shook her head. They drove on a bit further, but then he stopped again.

'Didn't you hear anything this time?' he asked.

No, she didn't and he drove on again. But when he stopped for the third time Mr Pepperpot said: 'You must have heard it; it sounded just like a cat miaowing.'

'Probably your brakes have got wet,' suggested Mrs Pepperpot.

'I'll have a look,' said Mr Pepperpot, and got out.

Mrs Pepperpot stayed where she was and stroked the kitten to keep him quiet. After a while she asked her husband if he'd found anything; she knew you shouldn't rush a man when he's looking for trouble in his car.

'Not yet!' came the answer from under the bonnet.

'Perhaps the engine is overheated?'

'Yes, I think I'll get some water from that farm up on the hill.' He took out a green plastic bucket and started trudging up the hill. He could see there was a pump in the front yard.

The farm was quite a long way off, so Mrs Pepperpot thought she could safely take a short stroll with the kitten. The little creature was very

good, running along beside her, purring and rubbing against her skirt.

'You have a better purr than the car engine,' said Mrs Pepperpot. 'Oh, look! There's a pigsty. Let's go and visit the pigs.'

Basking in the sunshine lay a big sow with a whole row of little piglets stretched out beside her. From time to time they woke up, pushed and nudged and sucked and squealed, then they fell asleep again.

Just as she was bending over to stroke the sow, lo and behold! Mrs Pepperpot SHRANK for the second time that day! This was most unusual and quite unexpected. Luckily, she didn't land among the pigs, but tumbled into a patch of weeds right by the sty.

'Did you hurt yourself? asked a squeaky little voice.

'No, I don't think so, thanks,' said Mrs Pepperpot, struggling to her feet. 'I'm so used to falling – it's almost second nature to me. Hullo! I thought I was talking to a kitten; now I see you're a pig!'

It was indeed a pig, but a very, very small and thin one.

'Don't you belong in there with the others?' asked Mrs Pepperpot.

'I do really. But the farmer put me out. He said my mother had enough to feed and I would have to fend for myself, unless . . .' The piglet put his head on one side and looked wistfully at Mrs Pepperpot from under his white eyelashes, ' . . . unless some nice person would take me home and feed me with a bottle.'

'Poor little mite! Does *nobody* want you?'

'Not so far. They all come and look at my mother and the others, gobbling away. But when they see me they just shake their heads and go away,' said the little pig.

'They're stupid and unkind!' said Mrs Pepperpot, 'leaving a fine little fellow like you to starve. I

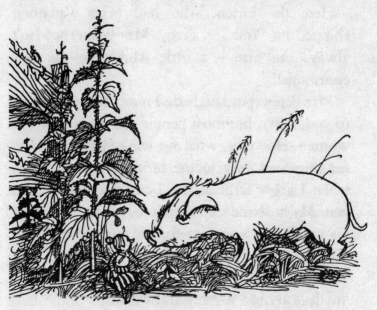

wish I had a bottle of milk handy. If I were my proper size, I'd take you home with me.'

Here the kitten, who had been watching, chipped in: 'You see, Piggy, Mrs Pepperpot isn't always this size – a little while ago she was enormous!'

Mrs Pepperpot laughed. 'I may seem enormous to you, Kitty, but most people call me a *little* old woman. However, what we want right now is to get ourselves over to the farmer's pump. Then, when I grow large again, I can ask if can have you. My husband's up there too, getting water for his car. But it's too far for me to walk as I am now.'

'I don't think I could carry you,' said the piglet, 'my legs are too wobbly and weak!'

'I'll do what I did before,' said the kitten, 'pull you along by your skirt.'

'Champion!' said Mrs Pepperpot. 'You wait here for us, Piggy. We may be some time, but we'll be back.'

They set off as before, the kitten tugging and pulling Mrs Pepperpot, bumping over the grass and stones. It was hard work up the hill, but the kitten didn't give up till they had reached the pump, where they found the green plastic bucket, but no Mr Pepperpot. He had gone inside to chat with the farmer about the wonders of his old car. They got so interested that when he came out he had forgotten what he came for – to fill his bucket with water.

Mrs Pepperpot, who had hidden inside the bucket when Mr Pepperpot and the farmer came

out of the house, wondered if she was going to be left behind. But halfway down the hill Mr Pepperpot remembered the bucket and came rushing back again. The farmer was still standing there: 'You won't get far without water!' he said, as Mr Pepperpot hitched the bucket under the pump and started pumping.

Poor Mrs Pepperpot! It wasn't very clever of her to hide in the bucket, was it? Now she was in great danger of drowning while Mr Pepperpot went on pumping and talking to the farmer at the same time.

'Travel broadens the mind,' he was saying. 'You need to get out and see for yourself what a beautiful country we live in. D'you know, when I sit behind that wheel with a long clear road in front of me, it often makes me want to sing and shout . . . *Ouch*!' And he gave a great shout and jumped in the air!

The farmer thought he was showing him what he did when he was driving, but Mr Pepperpot went on jumping about, the bucket fell off the hook and all the water ran out. And Mrs Pepperpot? Well, she had cleverly climbed out of the bucket and had managed to get a hold on Mr Pepperpot's trouser leg. Then, while he was still talking, she hoisted herself up as far as his braces, but there her foot slipped and she gave him a kick. She also pinched him while trying to stop herself from

falling. So that was why Mr Pepperpot shouted: he thought there was an ant inside his shirt.

By now all the rest of the family had come out of the house to look at this funny man dancing round their pump. When he saw they were laughing at him, he ran down the hill to find Mrs Pepperpot and get her to remove the ant, or whatever it was.

But there was no sign of Mrs Pepperpot either in the car or up and down the road.

'Oh dear, oh dear! Now she's shrunk and vanished completely. What shall I do?' After he had hunted around and called her in vain he suddenly remembered the ant. Heavens! That might have been her! He felt himself all over, but there was no sign of any creepy-crawly now. He would have to go back to the pump. Perhaps he could ask the farmer if he had seen his wife. But how was he going to explain that she might be as small as a tiny doll?

When he got to the pump the whole family was still standing there, so he laughed a little nervously and said: 'I came back for my bucket of water.'

They watched him pump it full again. Then he said: 'Oh, by the way, did you see if I dropped a small doll with a striped skirt on?'

'Doll?' said the farmer. 'No, I didn't see any doll. But I'll ask my wife. Have you seen the gentleman's doll, Kristina?'

'No,' said his wife, 'I didn't see any doll. But I'll ask my daughter.' She turned to the eldest girl: 'Have you seen a little doll, Gerda?'

'No,' said Gerda, 'I didn't see any doll. But I'll ask my younger sister, Britta. Did you see a little doll?'

'No,' said Britta, 'but I'll ask my smaller sister, Ada. Did you see a little doll?'

'No,' said Ada, 'but I'll ask my baby sister, Maggie. Did you see a little doll?'

'No,' said Maggie, 'but I'll ask my big brother, Jack. Did you see a little doll?'

'No,' said Jack, 'but I'll ask my bad brother, Ben. Did you see a little doll?'

'No,' said Ben, 'but I'll ask my good brother, Jim. Did you see a little doll?'

'No,' said Jim, 'but I'll ask my sad brother, Frank. Did you see a little doll?'

'No,' said Frank, 'but I'll ask my happy brother, Peter. Did you see a little doll?'

'No,' said Peter, 'but I'll ask my baby brother, John. Did you see a little doll?'

'No,' said Baby John. 'No lil dolly at all!'

'I'm afraid we haven't seen your doll,' said the farmer.

Meanwhile Mr Pepperpot was wringing his hands and muttering to himself: 'I've lost her – this time I really have lost my own dear wife!'

'Did you say *wife*?' asked the farmer with surprise. 'I thought it was a doll you had lost'

'Well, you see ... the doll ... er ...' Mr Pepperpot didn't know what to say.

'If it's your *wife* you're looking for,' said the farmer, slapping Mr Pepperpot on the back, 'don't

worry! We saw a little old lady in a striped skirt get into your car while you were on your way back here, didn't we, Kristina?'

'Yes,' said his wife, 'and my daughter saw her too, didn't you, Gerda?'

But before the whole family could go through their rigmarole again, Mr Pepperpot was off down the hill, not forgetting the green plastic bucket of water! When he got to the car, there sat Mrs Pepperpot, patiently waiting on the back seat, with her picnic basket on her knee.

Mr Pepperpot was so relieved, he gave her a big kiss. But he couldn't help asking her: 'Did you . . . did you SHRINK?'

'I don't know why you have to keep asking me about that, Mr P,' said Mrs Pepperpot crossly. 'Try and get that car going for a change!'

This time the car gave no trouble at all, of course. But Mr Pepperpot still felt it would be best to have it checked at the next garage, and Mrs Pepperpot didn't argue, as she wanted to go into the shop right beside it. There she bought a baby's bottle and teat and a pint of milk.

'What do you want that for?' asked her husband when she came back to the car.

'Questions! Questions! When are we going to get to that cross-country race you're so keen to go in for?'

'As a matter of fact, I don't think I *am* so keen now. The man here at the garage has just told me about a fair near here where they have one of those "trials of strength". You know: you hit an iron plate with a big hammer as hard as you can and a disc shoots up to ring a bell. I think I'd like to have a bash at that. You'd like to go to a fair, wouldn't you?'

'I expect so. I might try winning something myself,' said Mrs Pepperpot.

So off they went again: Mr Pepperpot, Mrs Pepperpot, one kitten and one piglet, which, up to now, had kept very quiet.

## III

They drove on for a while. Mr Pepperpot kept looking out for posters to show where the fair was being held. In the back seat Mrs Pepperpot had made up a little song to keep them amused. This is how it went:

'I know a little pussy-kitten,
With shiny coat and snowy mitten,
His ice-cream whiskers wrapped in a rug,
He's safe inside my basket snug.'

'I like to hear you sing,' said Mr Pepperpot, 'it shows you're feeling happy. I know the tune, too, but I don't remember those words:

'You're not likely to; I just made them up!' she answered. 'I'll sing you another verse:

'I know a little piggy pink,
With curly tail and eyes that twink,

> *His legs are shaky, but no one mocks,*
> *He likes to sit in my old box.'*

'It's a funny song, all right, and you're a funny old woman,' said Mr Pepperpot.

'Funny yourself' said his wife. 'Now I'll sing one about you. Here goes:

> *'I know a man who's not a giant,*
> *But very smart and self-reliant.*
> *In motoring he'd spend his life,*
> *He only fears to lose his wife!'*

'There!' shouted Mr Pepperpot, slowing down.

'Where? What?' Mrs Pepperpot didn't know what he was talking about.

'There's the fair. Now I can swing the Big Hammer – you'll see; I'll knock that thingummy right to the top – Ping! Let's see,' he got out and read the poster; 'there are lots of other attractions too; sword-swallowers and tightrope walkers . . .'

'I'd be careful about swallowing swords, if I were you,' said Mrs Pepperpot, getting out of the car and closing the door to keep her pets in. 'You make enough fuss if you get as much as a herring bone in your throat!'

'Silly! They're professionals! Well, I'm going this way to the Big Hammer. Why don't you go and look at the circus animals? They say they're as clever as people.' And with that Mr Pepperpot hurried off into the crowd.

The noise was terrific: hurdy-gurdy music from the merry-go-rounds, people screaming on the Big Wheel, Dodgems clanging and the stall-holders all trying to shout each other down.

Mrs Pepperpot felt quite lost, and wondered where she should go. She decided to buy another ice cream for the kitten and a carton of milk for that hungry piglet. He had been sleeping quietly in his box since she gave him the first bottle, but soon he'd be awake again, and then he might squeal and give the game away.

Just as she reached the kiosk, Mrs Pepperpot felt the ominous signs – 'Not again!' was all she had time to say before she shrank and found herself rolling on the ground with huge boots and shoes tramping all around her.

Was she scared! There was danger from every direction, and she was at her wits' end. Should she try to climb up someone's trouser – leg? Before she could make a grab, however, she found herself picked up by her skirt and whisked away from the

tramping feet. Whatever it was, it ran so fast that poor Mrs Pepperpot was slung from side to side and completely lost her breath. She tried to shout 'Let me go!', but then she realized it would be better to let herself get carried out of harm's way. Finally, behind a big tent, whatever-it-was stopped and she felt herself lowered carefully on to the grass. Looking up, she saw, standing over her, a furry creature with black, floppy ears and a big moustache.

'Hullo,' she said. 'What are you supposed to be?'

'Oh,' said the creature, 'I'm just me!'

Mrs Pepperpot laughed. 'I see! I ought to have known. Of course, you're a puppy. Perhaps you're one of those clever circus dogs trained to do tricks?'

'No one's going to train me to do tricks!'

declared the puppy, shaking his floppy ears vigorously. 'I do what I want and that's that!'

'Quite right,' said Mrs Pepperpot. 'I do what *I* want, too, except when I turn small like I am now. Then I have to rely on other people's help. If you can help me now, perhaps I can help *you* when I grow large. But I can only understand animal language when I am small, so if you've anything to tell me, you'd better do it now.'

Then the puppy told her his story in little excited barks. He really belonged to the circus manager, but when he wouldn't learn to count and to bark in the key of F major, the manager chased him out of his tent.

'But you haven't heard the worst,' added the puppy.

'Let's have it,' said Mrs Pepperpot.

The puppy put his head on one side and looked at her sadly. 'Are you pedigree?' he asked.

'Well,' laughed Mrs Pepperpot, 'I've never really thought about it. I don't think I care if I am or not.'

'As a dog, if you're not pedigree, you're useless, that's what they told me,' said the puppy.

'Never mind! You have a beautiful moustache.'

'They said it didn't belong with my kind of breed.'

'Bother them and their pedigree!' said Mrs Pepperpot. 'That moustache will come in very handy, for you and I are going to fool the whole lot of them!'

The puppy looked at her with big round eyes. 'Why, what are we going to do?'

'You must pick me up very carefully in your mouth, just like you did before,' said Mrs Pepperpot. 'And now jump straight on to the roof of that caravan!'

It was a most tremendous leap, but the puppy arrived safely with Mrs Pepperpot in his mouth. Then Mrs Pepperpot draped his long moustache over her skirts and legs, so that she was completely hidden. At first no one noticed them up there, but when the music stopped for a pause Mrs Pepperpot suddenly started to sing through the puppy's moustache:

> 'Baa, baa, black sheep,
> Here we go gathering nuts in May,

*Who killed Cock Robin?*
*Three blind mice, three blind mice,*
*Little Tommy Tucker,*
*Sing a song of sixpence,*
*Girls and boys come out to play,*
*See saw, Marjorie Daw.'*

Wasn't that an old jumble of a song? But it was
the best she could do, hanging there in mid-air.
The people standing round the caravan were
astonished to see a puppy on the roof, and even
more amazed that he was singing. Others joined
them to watch; the roundabout came to a halt,

the passengers left the Dodgems, and even the circus performance stopped as the audience flocked outside to hear the clever puppy sing.

The circus manager himself appeared. 'Hi!' he shouted, 'that's my puppy! Here, boy; here, boy!' But the puppy took no notice; it was all he could do to keep his balance with Mrs Pepperpot in his mouth.

'Can you count to ten?' shouted the circus manager. 'One?' No answer. 'Two!' Silence. 'Three? Four? Five?' Still no answer from the puppy. 'You're just having us on, you obstinate little brute! Six, seven, eight, nine, ten . . .'

Mrs Pepperpot decided it was time to teach the circus manager a lesson. In a high, yappy voice she said quickly: 'Eleven, twelve, thirteen, fourteen, fifteen, sixteen, seventeen, eighteen, nineteen, twenty!'

Consternation in the crowd! The circus manager jumped up and down, whooping with excitement. There was such a crush of people trying to see the puppy that they overturned the caravan and everyone fell on top of everyone else! When at last they had sorted themselves out, the puppy had disappeared. He and Mrs Pepperpot had jumped clear when the caravan toppled, and had made for the car as fast as his little legs could carry them.

When Mr Pepperpot returned, his wife, who was now her proper size, was wrapping something up in an old coat they kept in the back of the car.

Mr Pepperpot was so excited about the singing puppy, he didn't notice what she was doing. 'You should have heard him – he sang a whole song!'

Mrs Pepperpot laughed. 'Get along with you! A dog singing!'

'I saw him with my own eyes!' he assured her. Then he looked thoughtful for a moment and said: 'Come to think of it, it was rather like one of your daft songs!'

'Was it, indeed?' Mrs Pepperpot looked pained. 'How did you get on with the Big Hammer?'

'With all that fuss about the puppy, I didn't get time to try it. Anyway, I heard someone talking about a walking contest. So I thought I'd drive a little further and try that.'

'Very well,' said Mrs Pepperpot with a sigh. She was beginning to wonder if they'd ever get home that day; if they had to stay overnight somewhere, what would she do with the animals?

But Mr Pepperpot drove happily on, and in the back seat – though he didn't know it – he now had *four* passengers: Mrs Pepperpot, the kitten, the piglet and the puppy with black floppy ears and a big moustache.

# IV

When they had driven another few miles Mr Pepperpot stopped the car.

'I don't know what's wrong,' he said, 'but the car seems so heavy at the back. Perhaps the tyres are going flat; I expect I'd better pump them up a bit. You'll have to get out meanwhile.'

Mrs Pepperpot didn't like this idea. If her husband started rummaging in the back of the car he might find the animals.

'I don't feel like getting out just now,' she said. 'Can't it wait till you get to the next petrol station? Then they can do it for you.'

'I suppose so,' he said and drove on. But soon he was grumbling again: 'Why can't you sit still? If there's not enough room for you in the back seat, you could throw out some of that food.'

He didn't know that the food had been eaten up long ago by the piglet, the kitten and the puppy.

'If anything's to be thrown out, it's not the food!' said Mrs Pepperpot quite huffily. 'If your old car can't even carry one passenger, Mr P, *I* can get out, and you can go on alone!'

This was very cunning of Mrs Pepperpot, because if there is one thing a proud car-owner hates, it is criticism of his beautiful automobile.

'You stay right where you are!' said Mr Pepperpot. 'It's not really the weight that matters, but all the strange noises I have been hearing from the back. I must find out what's causing them.'

'Oh dear!' sighed Mrs Pepperpot, 'that must have been my singing you could hear. I was making up a sort of song – not a proper one, you understand, for *I* have never sung in a choir like *you* . . .'

Mr Pepperpot brightened up at the word 'choir', as he had been very good at choir-singing when he was young.

'That's right, my dear,' he said, 'not everyone is born with a beautiful voice. But you go right ahead and sing; nothing like it for uplifting the soul and making us think of the joys of spring!'

'Don't know so much about the joys of spring,' muttered Mrs Pepperpot, 'it's more like a farmyard when I get going. But you asked for it:

> *'Dogs are lots of fun,*
> *When they jump and run,*
> *But when they start to yap-yap,*
> *They will get a slap-slap!*
>
> *Cats are sweet and furry,*
> *Never in a hurry*
> *Till they start a row-row,*
> *Fight and scratch and miaow-miaow!*
>
> *As for little pigs,*
> *See them dancing jigs;*
> *Their little feet go boink-boink*
> *While their snouts go oink-oink!'*

'Ridiculous!' was Mr Pepperpot's comment. 'This time I didn't even know the tune.'

'Nor did I when I started,' said Mrs Pepperpot. 'I can see a petrol station over there.'

'Good,' said Mr Pepperpot. He stopped at the garage and asked the man to pump up his tyres, and Mrs Pepperpot hoped the animals would keep quiet meanwhile. But she needn't have worried, for her husband was soon deep in conversation with the garage man about a fishing competition which was due to start at two o'clock.

'You can put your name on this list,' the man was saying, 'and then I'll show you which way to go.'

Mr Pepperpot signed his name to show he was a competitor, and they set off again, this time down a narrow lane through a wood. It was lovely and cool in there and soon they got to a little green glade.

'This is where the man said I could park the car,' said Mr Pepperpot. He got out and fetched his fishing tackle from the boot. 'I suppose you don't want to come and watch me?'

'I'd rather wait for you to bring me back a lovely fish for my supper. I'll just lie in the nice grass and watch the trees for a bit.'

'Bye, bye, then,' said Mr Pepperpot, walking off towards the river, hopeful as ever.

Mrs Pepperpot called 'Good luck!' after him, but as soon as he was out of sight she opened the basket to let the kitten and the piglet out and

unrolled the puppy, who had been having a nice nap inside the old coat. They all came tumbling out on the grass. At first the kitten was a bit frightened and arched his back and hissed at the puppy, but soon they were all three chasing each other round and round. Mrs Pepperpot sat on a tree stump in the middle and enjoyed the fun. When she thought they had had enough exercise she caught them all and put them back in the car.

'Be good,' she told them. 'I'm going to the shop on the main road to buy some more food for you.' And she shut the car door securely.

It was very pleasant walking along the quiet lane, and she was quite sorry to get back on to the dusty road. Luckily, the shop wasn't far. It was one of those old-fashioned country stores where they sell everything from pickled herrings in

barrels to hair nets, barbed wire and liquorice. When she got there a lot of people were waiting to be served, so she took a stroll round the back where she found a chicken yard. She counted twelve fine hens, pecking and scraping in the sand, but over in a corner stood a miserable little bird, blinking her eyes and shivering. She looked so bedraggled and thin that Mrs Pepperpot at once felt sorry for her.

'You poor thing! But don't you worry; I'll have you out of here in no time, as sure as my name's Pepperpot!'

The little hen didn't seem to hear her, but Mrs Pepperpot went back inside and bought her provisions. When she had finished she asked the little man behind the counter if he would sell her the hen.

'Oh, you don't want that miserable creature!' he exclaimed. 'She's never been any good at laying eggs, and now she's getting old and tough too.'

'We none of us get any younger,' said Mrs Pepperpot, 'and she hasn't had much of a chance, being chased round the yard from morning till night.' As you know, when Mrs Pepperpot makes up her mind she can be very determined, and at last the little man gave in. He found a big cardboard box and put the hen in it. She was so scared she lay absolutely still.

Mrs Pepperpot left the shop with the cardboard box under one arm and the basket of food under the other. It was quite a heavy load for her to carry, and when she reached the lane she put both down, so that she could change hands and have a rest. Also she wanted to see if the hen was all right. She lifted the lid just a little.

'Mercy!' she shouted, for at that moment she SHRANK for the *fourth* time that day and toppled in with the hen!

More frightened than ever, the bird flapped out of the box, but Mrs Pepperpot managed to cling on to one of her legs. This stopped the hen from flying away.

'Woah!' said Mrs Pepperpot. 'Stand still while I get on your back.' The hen was squawking, and as soon as Mrs Pepperpot was on her back she ran as fast as she could into the bushes, where she got stuck.

'You're a scatterbrain and no mistake!' Mrs Pepperpot told her when they were out in the lane again.

'That's what they've all said – ever since I was born,' said the hen sadly.

Mrs Pepperpot patted her neck. 'I'm sorry, I didn't mean to hurt your feelings. Don't you bother what people say. From now on you're coming to live with me and be my very special feathered friend.'

'Thanks very much, but would you tell me where we are going and how we are going to get anywhere with you such a very small person?'

'Quite right, I should have said. I want you to take me along this lane till we get to my husband's car. I'm not this size all the time, you see, and should be back to normal human size soon.'

'Well, I hope you hurry up, because I can see the fox over there in the bushes!' said the hen, blinking her eyes nervously in that direction. Sure enough! There stood Master Fox, and he was licking his chops.

'Don't worry,' whispered Mrs Pepperpot, 'I'll deal with him!' Out loud she said: 'I see a certain well-known person is out for a walk in the sunshine.'

'That's right. I was giving myself an appetite for my dinner. And I seem to be in luck,' laughed the fox, 'as my dinner is out walking too!' And he made ready to spring on the hen.

'Hold on!' shouted Mrs Pepperpot. 'Don't be in too much of a hurry, Master Fox. You see, I'm going round with invitations to a picnic, so I may as well invite you too. That is, if you'll behave like a gentleman.'

'Very funny!' said the fox, showing his teeth. 'Of course you thought you could trick me like the cockerel once did when he got me to wash my paws before I started eating. I know that one!' He put one paw on the hen, who was trembling all over by now.

But Mrs Pepperpot kept calm. 'I'm not trying to trick you,' she said. 'If you'll let go of the hen at once I promise you'll have a meal much better than a tough old bird. But first I want you to carry the basket of groceries over to that car in the glade. Then you can come back and fetch me and the hen.'

'Oh no!' cackled the hen, more terrified than ever.

'Another trick!' said the fox. 'When I get back you'll both be gone. I want my food *now*!' He put the other paw on Mrs Pepperpot's skirt.

'How stupid you are!' said Mrs Pepperpot. 'I've always heard that foxes were so smart, but that must have been in the old days. If you're afraid of losing us, the hen can carry me on her back and we'll walk beside you all the way.'

The fox agreed. He took the basket in his mouth and the hen carried Mrs Pepperpot on her back till they reached the car. Once there,

Mrs Pepperpot asked the fox to unpack the food and sent the hen up on the roof of the car to fetch a plastic tablecloth which they spread on the grass.

'When do we start the feast!' asked the fox.

'We'll have to wait till I collect the rest of the guests,' said Mrs Pepperpot. Then she put her hand to her mouth and shouted with all her might: 'Are you there, Great Cat Tiger-claws?'

'Miaow!' said a little voice from the car.

'What's this?' demanded the fox. 'Are there other guests invited?'

'Oh yes!' answered Mrs Pepperpot, putting her hand to her mouth again. 'Are you there, Wild Boar Gory Fangs?' she shouted as loudly as she could.

'Oink! Oink!' came the reply from the car.

'Good heavens! Are there any more?' The fox was beginning to look nervous.

'Wait and see!' said Mrs Pepperpot. 'Are you there, Handlebar Moustachio Foxhunter?'

'Woof! Woof!' answered the puppy.

'Thanks very much,' said the fox. 'I don't think I fancy this picnic after all!'

'Oh, come on! They'll all be very pleased to see you,' said Mrs Pepperpot. 'You just sit down and enjoy yourself. The hen can sit next to you if you like.'

'I'd rather not!' said the poor hen, who didn't trust the fox one inch.

The fox looked hurt. 'You've tricked me just like the others,' he said. But Mrs Pepperpot shook her head:

'No. I promised you food, and I keep my promises. You can put a large chunk of ham and some fresh eggs in the basket and take it away to eat. Will that satisfy you?'

'Very generous, I'm sure,' said the fox, collecting the food in the basket and picking it up .

Just as he was about to run off with it, Mrs Pepperpot said: 'Just a minute! One thing more. I want the basket back.'

'All right,' said the fox, 'if you can keep your promises, I can keep mine . I'll see you get it back.' With that he vanished in the bushes, much to the hen's relief.

At that moment Mrs Pepperpot grew to her proper size. She lost no time in getting her pets out and they all had a lovely picnic in the grass. She had just finished putting them back in their different hiding places when Mr Pepperpot returned from his fishing contest. But she could see from his face that there would be no fish for supper *that* night.

'What happened?' she asked.

'Oh,' he said despondently, 'it wasn't much of a turnout. We had an hour for the contest, but I never got a single bite. And then something very strange happened.'

'What was that?'

'Well, you see this basket?' He held up a basket, still wet. 'D'you recognise it?'

'It's our picnic basket,' she said.

'That's right! What I want to know is: how did it come to be floating downstream towards me when you are here, much further down the river?' Mr Pepperpot was scratching his head and looking very puzzled.

Mrs Pepperpot could hardly stop herself from laughing, but she just said: 'I have no idea! How did you get it back?'

'It floated straight on to my line, so I hooked it out.'

'Life's full of surprises, isn't it?' said Mrs Pepperpot, getting back in the car. 'Now let's get on, Mr P, or we'll never get home today.'

So Mr Pepperpot turned the car out of the little glade and drove off with Mrs Pepperpot, the kitten, the piglet, the puppy and the hen all on the back seat.

## V

They had not gone many miles when Mr Pepperpot put his foot on the brake and stopped very sharply.

'*Now* what's up?' asked Mrs Pepperpot, who had been having a little doze.

'There's a poster about a contest,' said Mr Pepperpot. 'I want to see what it says.'

'Don't you think we've had enough contests for today? We're getting tired and it's time to go home.'

'Speak for yourself, Mrs P. – I'm not tired,' said Mr Pepperpot.

'Anyway, I wish you wouldn't put the brakes on so suddenly, you should think of us in the back seat,' said Mrs Pepperpot.

'Us? Who's us?' he asked.

'Why . . . er . . . the baggage and me!' Mrs Pepperpot was a little flustered – she had nearly given the game away! But her husband had now got out of the car to look at the poster, and this is what it said:

SENSATIONAL SPORTS EVENT TODAY
The Great Traditional Cross-Country Race
starting from Railway Square at 4 p.m.
The Course is as Follows:
Cross Bilberry Marsh by mapped-out Route,
Wade over Black River above the Waterfall,
Take 12 ft Leap from Red Cliff on the North
bank to White Rock on the South bank. Run to
finishing line at the Big Spruce Tree.
1st Prize a Silver Cup.
Refreshments Served.

'Mercy me!' said Mrs Pepperpot when her husband read it out. 'You're never thinking of entering that one, are you?'

'Well, I don't know,' he said. 'I'd like to watch it anyway.'

'And what are we going to do meanwhile?' she asked.

Mr Pepperpot stared at her. 'You said "we" again!'

'Oh well!' she said crossly, 'you keep stopping and starting, and messing about – is it any wonder if I get mixed up? What am *I* going to do, then? Sit in this stuffy old car?'

'No. As you say you're tired, I'll drop you at the station and you take the train home.'

Mrs Pepperpot thought this over, but then she agreed. 'As long as you leave the car in the station yard and promise me not to take part in the stupid competition,' she said.

He promised and drove the car to the station, where he parked it. He gave Mrs Pepperpot some money to get home and then he went round the other side to the Railway Square to watch the competitors line up for the race.

When he was out of sight Mrs Pepperpot went over to the ticket office. There she bought a ticket for herself and paid for the animals to be put in a

wooden crate, so that they could travel in the guard's van. A nice guard helped her get the animals in.

'I'll stay with them till the train comes,' she told the guard, and sat down on the crate. But just as the train pulled up at the platform poor Mrs Pepperpot did her fifth SHRINKING for that day! The crate had wide gaps between the boards, and Mrs Pepperpot fell straight through on to the kitten's tail!

'Miaow!' said the kitten, 'that hurt!'

'Sssh! Don't make a noise,' said Mrs Pepperpot, 'just try and hide me – I don't want the guard to see me like this!'

The animals did their best: the kitten curled his tail over her dress, the puppy spread one ear over her blouse and the hen held one wing carefully over her face. The pig just stretched out beside her and blinked at her from under his white eyelashes. When the guard came back he lifted the crate into the guard's van. Then he looked round for the old woman. Where could she have gone? It was only a little train, so he looked into all the carriages and asked the stationmaster if he had seen her. She was nowhere.

But the train couldn't wait, so the guard blew his whistle and off they went. The animals were

delighted to have Mrs Pepperpot with them. 'How lucky you shrank just now!' they said.

'Well, you'd better make the most of me while you have me,' she told them. 'After five shrinkings in one day I don't suppose it will happen again for a long time. So, if you have any questions, fire away!'

The animals all lined up like a row of school children with Mrs Pepperpot as their very small teacher standing out in front.

The kitten began: 'Please, ma'am, when do we get to your house?'

'In time for supper,' said Mrs Pepperpot firmly, but to herself she added 'I hope', for she wondered what would happen when they got to their station.

'What am I going to have to eat?' asked the piglet.

'Don't worry, there's a whole bin of lovely mash for piglets at my house,' she assured him.

'What about dogs?' asked the puppy. 'Can I do as I like?'

'Certainly!' said Mrs Pepperpot. 'Liberty Hall, that's what they call my place!'

The hen looked anxiously at her. 'Will there be a lot of other hens in your yard? Will they peck me?'

'You shall be my one and only special hen; didn't I tell you?' said Mrs Pepperpot.

All the animals clapped and flapped and stamped and shouted: 'Hooray for Mrs Pepperpot!'

To keep them from getting too boisterous and to while away the time she decided to teach them a song. 'Listen carefully,' she said, 'and come in when I point to you.' She began to sing:

> *'Children all, now gather round,*
> *And let us make a jolly sound,*
> *First a dog and then a cat,*
> *A little pig, a hen, all pat!*
>
> *Here we go: sing as I do,*
> *Puppy dog, a bark from you!*
> *Woof, woof! Woof, woof!'*

Here she pointed to the puppy and he barked as loudly as he could: 'Woof, woof! Woof, woof!'

*'Here we go: sing as I do,*
*Little Puss, a song from you!*
*Miaow, miaow! Miaow, miaowl'*

The kitten didn't wait to be asked, but sang in chorus with Mrs Pepperpot: 'Miaow, miaow! Miaow, miaow!'

*'Here we go: sing as I do,*
*Piglet, we must hear from you!*
*Oink, oink! Oink, oink!'*

When Mrs Pepperpot pointed at him, the piglet got so carried away, he wouldn't stop 'oinking', and the puppy had to give him a sharp nip.

*'Here we go: sing as I do,*
*Hennypen, a cluck from you!*
*Cluck, cluck! Cluck, cluck!'*

But the hen was so frightened by all the noise the others had made, she only managed a very small 'cluck, cluck!' the first time. However, they went on practising, and by the time the train stopped at their station they were all singing very well indeed.

The guard opened the door and lifted the crate on to a trolley with a lot of milk churns. As nobody else got out of the train he blew the whistle and it moved off. Luckily Mrs Pepperpot's name and address were written on the lid, so when Peter, the milkman, came in his van to fetch the churns he saw the crate and thought he was meant to deliver it together with the milk. This saved Mrs Pepperpot a lot of trouble, for as soon as he had put the crate down at the corner of the road leading to her house, and had driven off, there was an almighty CRASH!

Mrs Pepperpot grew so fast that she burst right through the crate, scattering the animals and the boards pell-mell all around. Such a to-do! The hen landed on the branch of a tree, the puppy rolled down the hill, the piglet got his snout stuck in a hole and the poor kitten fell in the stream!

When Mrs Pepperpot had picked herself up she quickly collected all the animals. She put the hen under one arm and the piglet under the other and called the kitten and the puppy to follow her. All together they climbed the hill to her house.

'Here we are, children, home at last!' she said, as she opened the door, and set the hen and the piglet down. The kitten and the puppy trotted in after her and now they were all nosing round to see what their new house was like.

Mrs Pepperpot sat down. She had a problem. Mr Pepperpot was bound to come home soon. How was she going to tell him about the additions to their family? She put her finger on her nose and thought. Then she cried: 'I've got it! I have a solution!'

First she put the kitten in the bed and covered him with the counterpane. Then she put the piglet in the empty wood box by the stove and sprinkled wood shavings all over him. The puppy she hid in a basket under the table, and the hen she lifted up on the bureau. 'You keep very still,' she told her, 'I'm going to cover you up.' And she put a large lampshade over her. Then she put the coffee on and went outside to see if her husband was coming.

There he was, struggling up the hill, looking so downcast that she had to shout and wave to him to let him know she was there. When he did see her his whole face lit up and he fairly sprinted up the last bit of the road.

'Am I glad you're here!' he said, giving her a big kiss.

'Why shouldn't I be here, Mr P?' said Mrs Pepperpot. 'What have you done with the car?'

'I couldn't very well take it through the bog and jump it over the river, could I?'

Mrs Pepperpot threw up her hands in horror: 'You never went in for that race, did you? After promising . . . ?'

'I know. I only meant to watch it. But then I heard the railway guard asking people if they'd seen a little old woman who was supposed to be travelling on the train to our station. He said she'd disappeared. So, of course, I thought at once it must be you who had turned small.'

'What happened then?' she asked.

'Well, I tried to jump on the train, which was just pulling out, but I couldn't catch it. So I headed straight for Bilberry Marsh. I knew it was a short cut and it would have taken much longer to drive the car round by the road.'

'Go on!' said Mrs Pepperpot, all ears.

'The path across the marsh was clearly marked for the race and it took me straight to the place above the waterfall where you have to wade across. Then I scrambled down the other side till I got to Red Cliff.'

Mrs Pepperpot's eyes were popping out of her head by now: 'You didn't take the twelve-foot leap to White Rock, did you?'

'Of course I did; there was no other way!'

'Then you must have won the race!' said Mrs Pepperpot. 'Did they give you the Prize Cup?'

'I didn't wait for anything like that. All I was thinking about was getting to the station in time to get you out of the train. But I was too late and I thought I'd never see you again.'

'Silly!' said Mrs Pepperpot, but she was wiping her eyes with her apron and sniffing a little. 'Come on in and have some coffee.'

When he was sitting comfortably with his cup of coffee she patted his cheek and said: 'Thanks for the outing. I enjoyed it!'

He smiled. 'I'm glad! And you didn't shrink, did you?'

'Well . . . er . . . actually I did – five times in all.'

'You SHRANK FIVE TIMES!!!' Mr Pepperpot looked thunderstruck.

Mrs Pepperpot decided to tell him the whole story: 'The first time I was very frightened in case you should leave me behind.'

'You know I'd never do that!' said Mr Pepperpot.

She smiled at him. 'No, you wouldn't, would you? Not many people have such kind husbands as *I* have. Well, the first time I shrank I met a kitten. The family he belonged to had gone back to town and left him – just like that – with no food or shelter. Would you have done that?'

'No indeed, that's a terrible thing to do!' said Mr Pepperpot.

'I knew that's how you would feel. So I thought it best to take the kitten along with me. Pussy! Pussy! You can come out now and meet your new master!'

'Miaow!' said the kitten and stuck his little head out from the bedclothes.

'Well, I'll be . . . !' said Mr Pepperpot. But Mrs Pepperpot was already hurrying him back into the kitchen.

'The second time I shrank,' she said, 'I met a piglet. That was when you went to get water from the pump, remember?'

'So it *was* you and not an ant climbing up my trouser leg?'

'It was. But never mind that. The little pig had been thrown out by the farmer to fend for himself, and he was so miserable I *had* to help him. I mean, *I've* never had to go hungry in my life – have you?'

'Well, no, I suppose I haven't ...' said Mr Pepperpot, scratching his head.

'There, you see, I knew you would agree. Come on, Piggy, show yourself to Mr Pepperpot!' And out of the shavings in the wood box came first a

pair of pink ears, then a little pink snout and lastly a whole pink piglet.

'Good gracious!' said Mr Pepperpot.

'But that's not all,' said his wife. 'The third time I shrank was at the fair. There I was, right on the ground under all those people's feet . . .'

Mr Pepperpot was holding his ears. 'Stop! Don't tell me! One of these days you'll get yourself killed.'

'Ah, but I was rescued by a very clever puppy, one that had you all gasping with his singing and his counting.'

'No! You don't mean to say that that was you as well?'

Mrs Pepperpot nodded. 'But I think it's more important that a dog should be a real dog and not

learn circus tricks – a dog that can be your friend
and protect you.'

'You mean we ought to have a guard dog?' said
Mr Pepperpot.

'That's right, and I have the very one. Out you
come, Puppy! Show your master how clever
you are!'

'Woof! Woof!' barked the puppy excitedly, as
he danced round Mr Pepperpot's feet.

'You see, he's your friend already,' said Mrs
Pepperpot, as her husband bent down to pat the
floppy black ears and pull that long moustache.

'Good dog!' he said.

'The fourth time was when you were fishing. I had gone to the shop for some groceries, and I bought a hen because she didn't lay eggs.'

'Because she *didn't* lay eggs?' Mr Pepperpot was getting quite confused.

'Well no, you see, she was being henpecked by all the other birds in the yard, so she didn't really have a chance!'

'Cluck-cluck-cluck-aloooooh!' The sound came from under the lampshade. Mrs Pepperpot hurried to take it off, and there stood the hen on the bureau, and under her lay a large, brown egg!

Mr Pepperpot burst out laughing: 'She's certainly making up for lost time!'

'She laid it specially for you!' said Mrs Pepperpot, 'because you're the kindest and most

understanding of husbands, and all the animals love you!'

'Steady on!' protested Mr Pepperpot. 'You know very well it's you the animals love. You must have the first egg!'

'I don't care what you say, this one's going to be fried for you!' And she cracked it on the edge of the frying pan while Mr Pepperpot watched. Into the hot fat fell two golden yolks!

'That hen knows how to keep the peace,' said Mr Pepperpot, 'now we can each have an egg!'

When they had had their supper Mrs Pepperpot said: 'I have one more surprise for you.'

Mr Pepperpot groaned: 'Not another animal, I hope.'

'Come into the parlour and I'll show you,' she said and opened the door. There on the table stood a brightly polished silver cup.

'That's for you!' she said. 'You've certainly earned it today.'

'But that's the cup you won for handling livestock when you were a young girl working on the farm!'

'Well, I give it to you now because you're just as good at handling livestock!' answered Mrs Pepperpot.

'I suppose we could hold it jointly . . . ?' suggested Mr Pepperpot.

'That's a very good idea. And now, have you thought what you will do with the rest of your holiday?' she asked him.

'I can't say I have, but I don't think I'll do any more motoring.'

'Good!' said Mrs Pepperpot, 'I think it's very nice to stay at home sometimes. And then you can get out your toolbox and build a pen for the piglet, a run for the hen, a kennel for the dog and . . .'

'And *nothing* for the cat!' said Mr Pepperpot firmly. But the kitten didn't mind; he was already stretched out in his favourite spot – along the top of Mr Pepperpot's armchair.

# Mrs Pepperpot has a Visitor
# from America

IT'S NOT so often that there's a letter in the post for Mrs Pepperpot. But one day when she opened her letter box she found a big letter with many foreign stamps on it. It was from her sister who lives in St Paul, Minnesota, USA, and this is what it said:

*Dear Sister,*
  *I am now on my way to the Old Country and would like to visit you. Can you come and meet me at Fornebu Airport? That will make me very, very happy.*

*Your loving sister, Margret Anne*

'Well, well!' said Mrs Pepperpot to herself, 'so my loving sister is coming back to Norway? It must be forty years since we last saw each other and there wasn't much loving sister about her then. As I remember it, I always got the short end of the stick. We'd go to the store and it would be little me to carry the basket while Miss Hoity Toity Margret Anne talked with the boys. And at school . . . I shall never forget the day she said I'd spilt ink over her copybook and ruined it. As if I'd do a thing like that! Then there was the other time she fell in the brook and said I'd pushed her in. If we went blueberry picking she'd pinch my basket because it was full and she was too lazy to get her own. And then . . .'

But we won't go on listening to all this miserable stuff, because it's quite clear that Mrs Pepperpot was in a very bad mood that day. All the same, her sister would have to be met at the airport; there was no getting away from that!

'I'll go,' said Mrs Pepperpot, 'but if Margret Anne thinks I'm going to doll myself up for her sake, she's much mistaken! I'll put on some old clothes of our mother's and a shawl round my head, and I'll take my broom along. Then my fine sister may not even want to know me!'

The day came and Mrs Pepperpot took the bus to the airport. It was quite a long trip and the other passengers were a bit surprised to see her get on in her old-fashioned clothes and carrying a broom.

At the airport there was a great crowd of people, and they stared even more at the little old woman with her shawl and her broom. Some of them were talking in foreign languages, and everyone was carrying heavy suitcases and pushing this way and that. By the time the loudspeaker announced that the plane from New York was about to land, Mrs Pepperpot was so confused, she didn't know if she was standing on

her head or her heels. As it happened, it didn't matter very much, because at that moment she SHRANK!

'Oh my goodness!' wailed Mrs Pepperpot, as she rolled along the slippery floor and very nearly got trodden on. 'What a time for this to happen!'

But almost at once she felt herself snatched up by a large lady's hand and popped into a glass showcase.

'Somebody must have been trying to steal one of the souvenirs,' said the large lady and locked the door of the showcase.

There stood Mrs Pepperpot, shawl, broom and all! She could see the people coming in from the plane, and among them, looking anxiously round, was a lady in a smart fawn hat and flowers on her coat and dress which matched the flowers on her outsize handbag. She wore spectacles with jewelled rims which sparkled most amazingly.

'That must be Margret Anne,' thought Mrs Pepperpot, and a moment later she was sure, because the lady walked past the showcase talking aloud to herself:

'Oh dear, where can my sister be? I'd better wait a bit.'

She came back and looked into the showcase.

'Maybe I should buy some Norwegian souvenirs for my friends in America. Oh, what a wonderful doll! She looks just like my mother with that shawl, and she used to have a broom just like that. But the face isn't like her – oh no, it has such a bad-tempered expression!'

Mrs Pepperpot was fuming inside: 'Has it indeed! I wonder what your mother would say if she could see *you*, dressed up as you are, in your American finery!'

Margret Anne went on talking to herself: 'I really must buy that doll to show my sister; she'll think it very, very funny!'

Mrs Pepperpot didn't think it funny at all, but held herself as stiff as she could while the large lady picked her up and gave her to Margret Anne, who paid for her and put her in her outsize handbag. Before it was closed, Mrs Pepperpot had time to see what a lot of knick-knacks there were inside: powder compact, lipsticks, paper hankies, face cream, notebooks, pens and pencils, cigarettes . . . Once the lid was closed Mrs Pepperpot was almost suffocated with all the different smells and she badly wanted to sneeze. But she kept as still as a mouse while her sister called a taxi.

Margret Anne told the taxi-man to drive all the way to the valley where Mrs Pepperpot lived, which was many miles away.

'That'll cost her a pretty penny!' thought Mrs Pepperpot. 'But at least I'll get a free ride.'

The taxi drove on and on, and Mrs Pepperpot must have had a little snooze, because suddenly she woke up to hear her sister say: 'Driver! Stop at this shop, please! I haven't been here since I was a child, and I want to go in and buy a few things for my sister. When she was a little girl she was always so good about carrying the groceries home for me.'

'Well, I never!' said Mrs Pepperpot inside the handbag.

Margret Anne went up to the counter and bought some smoked fish, some goat-milk cheese and some strong Norwegian sausage.

'I haven't tasted these things for forty years,' she told the grocer, who was a young man and didn't remember Margret Anne. She put all the things in her handbag on top of poor Mrs Pepperpot.

'Pooh!' said Mrs Pepperpot. 'I'll die if I have to stay in this smelly bag much longer!'

Just as she was going out of the shop, Margret Anne asked the grocer if he had a small bottle of ink.

'Good gracious! What does she want that for?' thought Mrs Pepperpot, as the ink bottle was poked into a corner beside her.

Then she heard her sister ask the taxi-man to drive to the schoolhouse.

'I want to look at the room where my sister and I learned our lessons. It's all so long ago, but

I've often thought how unkind I was when I told the teacher my sister poured ink on my copy-book.'

'I see!' thought Mrs Pepperpot. 'The bottle of ink is a peace offering. Better late than never!'

When she had looked inside the little old school-room, Margret Anne asked the driver to stop a short way out of the village where there was a bridge over the brook.

'You see, that's where I once fell in when I was a child and I told my mother that my sister pushed me.'

'I got a good hiding for that, my fine lady!' said Mrs Pepperpot inside the bag.

'I'd like to sit on the bridge for a moment and think about how wicked I was. D'you think my sister will have forgiven me?'

The taxi-man laughed: 'Why, ma'am,' he said, 'she'll be so pleased to see you after all these years, she won't worry about your little tiffs when you were young!'

'Perhaps she's not so bad, after all,' thought Mrs Pepperpot.

Margret Anne was dangling her legs over the edge of the bridge and staring down into the water, when suddenly she saw a great fish swimming by.

She got so excited, she dropped the handbag into the brook!

'Help, help!' cried Mrs Pepperpot, as the bag went whirling downstream. She was rolling round and round inside with the cheese and the fish and, worst of all, the ink! The cap had come off and she was covered in the stuff. Luckily the bag hit a stone which forced the catch open and Mrs Pepperpot was thrown out.

Remembering a diving lesson a frog had given her once, she went in head first to clean off the

ink, and then she swam to the bank, pulling the bag after her.

'Now if only I could get back to my proper size!' she said, and, for once, it actually happened as she wished.

She was not far from home, so she ran up the hill as fast as she could go and into her house.

When Margret Anne arrived a few minutes later in the taxi, there stood her sister to greet her at the door, wearing a nice clean frock and with her hair neatly combed.

'Aw, honey! It's good to see my little sister after all these years!' cried Margret Anne, as she flung her arms round Mrs Pepperpot's neck.

'Little is right,' thought Mrs Pepperpot, but all she said was: 'You're very welcome, Margret Anne, I'm sure.' She could see the taxi-man was grinning as he turned the car down the hill.

'Come on in and make yourself at home!' she went on, and led her sister indoors where the table was laid with strawberry layer-cake and pancakes with blueberry jam.

Margret Anne walked round admiring everything and saying how wonderful it was to be home. Then she remembered the lost handbag.

'It just fell out of my hand,' she told Mrs Pepperpot, 'and the water was running so fast it disappeared before we could catch it, though the driver did his best. I had everything in it, except my money, but what I'm really sorry about, honey, was a little old doll, dressed in a long black skirt with a shawl over its head and carrying a broom. It looked so like our mother – you'd have died laughing!'

'Is this the handbag!' asked Mrs Pepperpot, shyly holding up a large wet object that was still dripping on the floor. 'I got out of it – I mean, I *found* it – just down below the hill. But the doll has gone, I'm afraid.'

'How sad!' said Margret Anne, 'and the bag is a wreck!'

To console her sister, Mrs Pepperpot brought
out one of those plastic dolls, dressed in the latest
American fashion and with a pair of jewelled
spectacles on just like Margret Anne. How they
both laughed! And as they were hungry after all
their adventures, they sat down to eat the delicious
pancakes and layer-cake.

'I haven't tasted anything so good for forty
years,' declared Margret Anne. Then she looked
at Mrs Pepperpot and said: 'It's funny, sister, but
I always thought of you as such a small person.'

Mrs Pepperpot grinned: 'There are times when
I feel pretty small myself!'

# Mrs Pepperpot and the
# Budgerigar

NEAR Mrs Pepperpot's house stands a very
pretty little cottage with a garden round it.
There is also a handsome double gate decorated with
trees and flowers and leaves, all made of wrought
iron and painted shiny black. Entwined in the
leaves on one side of the gate is the word 'Happy'
and on the other the word 'Home'. So when the
gate is shut it reads 'Happy Home'. As a matter
of fact, the cottage belongs to a Mr and Mrs
Happy. The wife's first name is Bella, but no one's
ever heard the husband's first name, as he hardly
ever speaks to anyone, but just sits under the
sunshade in the garden and reads his newspaper.

Mrs Pepperpot thinks 'Mr Glum' would have suited him better.

The Happys are only there in the summer holidays, but then Mrs Pepperpot sees quite a lot of Mrs Happy. She pops over to borrow a bit of rhubarb or a cup of flour, or to snip a few chives or some parsley. This goes on nearly every day, and they always have a little chat and then Mrs Happy says: 'You really must come and visit *me* one of these days and meet my Pipkins – he is such a darling bird!'

Pipkins is Mrs Happy's budgerigar, which she brings with her from town, so that he too can have a nice country holiday.

'He's getting so clever at talking,' said Mrs Happy one day. 'I've taught him to say four whole words now. As soon as I have a free day, Mrs Pepperpot, I'll invite you over.'

Mrs Pepperpot had never seen a budgerigar and was very curious to hear a bird talking, so she thanked Mrs Happy and hoped she'd soon be asked.

But the days went by, and although Mrs Happy still kept coming over for this and that which she'd forgotten to buy at the store, she always seemed to be too busy to invite Mrs Pepperpot to her house.

Then one morning Mrs Pepperpot had been picking sugar peas for her husband's supper and she found she had quite a lot over.

'I could take them over to Mrs Happy,' she said to herself. 'Then perhaps she would let me have a look at that budgery-thing-e-me-jig. I'd dearly like to hear a bird talk.'

So she put on her best apron and scarf, popped the peas in a paper bag and walked over to 'Happy Home'. She went through the wrought-iron gate, up the path and through the open front door. Inside the hall she knocked on one of the closed doors. No one answered, but she could hear

Mrs Happy talking to someone inside. 'Come on, darling,' she was saying, 'just to please me, say "Thank you, Mama!"'

'That's funny,' thought Mrs Pepperpot, 'I never knew Mrs Happy had any children.' She knocked again.

'Wait a minute, my love,' said Mrs Happy inside, 'there's someone at the door.' And she opened the door just a tiny crack.

'Oh, it's you, Mrs Pepperpot,' she said, slipping through the door and shutting it behind her. 'How kind of you to call.'

'I just brought you these peas from the garden,' said Mrs Pepperpot and handed her the bag.

'Thank you so much; I love sugar peas!' said Mrs Happy. 'I wish I could ask you in, but just now I'm busy with my little boy . . .'

'You never told me you had a son,' said Mrs Pepperpot.

Mrs Happy laughed. 'Oh dear, no, I mean my Pipkins, my little budgie! He's all I have, you know, and just now I'm making him practise the words he can say, so that my friends can hear him when they come to tea this afternoon. They're coming all the way from town.'

'Well, I'll be going then,' said Mrs Pepperpot, who was a bit disappointed at not being asked in.

'Come round tomorrow morning,' said Mrs Happy, 'and have a cup of coffee and help me finish up the cakes.'

When she got home Mrs Pepperpot remembered that she hadn't time next morning, as that was her washing day.

'I'll slip over later and tell her I can't come,' she said to herself. So, about three o'clock, she walked over to the cottage and again she found the front door open, so she went into the hall and knocked on one of the inner doors. As there was no reply, she opened the door and found herself in the sitting-room. It was all ready for the tea party, she could see, with a pretty white cloth on the table, the best china set out and a big vase of flowers. On a smaller table by the window stood a cage.

Mrs Pepperpot couldn't resist going over to have a look at the pretty blue bird which was swinging to and fro on its perch. She sat down on the table beside the cage and said: 'Hullo, Pipkins, are you going to talk to me?'

The bird just looked at her.

'I don't believe it *can* talk!' said Mrs Pepperpot, and as she said that she felt herself SHRINK!

'So you don't believe I can talk,' said the budgerigar, but now, of course, he was talking bird language, which Mrs Pepperpot could understand when she grew small.

'Well,' said Mrs Pepperpot, 'I hadn't *heard* you talking till now.' She was standing on the table, wondering how she was going to get away before Mrs Happy and her guests came in.

'As a matter of fact,' said the bird, 'you've come just at the right moment. I want you to help me.'

'Help *you*? How can I help you when I don't even know how to help myself just now?' said Mrs Pepperpot, walking all round the cage to see

if there was anything she could climb down by.
But she was trapped!

'Well, I want to play a trick on Mrs Happy,'
said the bird.

'A trick, Pipkins, what sort of a trick?' asked
Mrs Pepperpot.

'Please don't call me by that stupid name.
Pipkins, indeed; my real name is "Suchislife".

Don't you think that sounds more superior?' The budgerigar was preening his feathers as he spoke, and looking down his beak at Mrs Pepperpot.

'Oh yes,' she said hurriedly, 'very superior!' Secretly she thought it sounded like something her husband usually said when he hadn't won the ski race: 'Ah well, such is life!'

'What d'you want me to do?' she asked the bird.

'I'll explain,' said Suchislife. 'But we must be quick, as Mrs Happy has only gone down the hill to meet her guests. First, will you open the door of the cage, please?'

Mrs Pepperpot did as she was asked and unhinged the cage door.

'Now, just step inside,' went on the bird, and Mrs Pepperpot walked into the cage.

No sooner was she in than the budgerigar hopped out and, quick as lightning, fastened the door-hinge with his beak!

'Got you!' he chirped merrily and flapped his wings with excitement.

Mrs Pepperpot glared at him through the bars. 'You needn't think you can be funny with me!' she said, 'or I shall take back my offer to help!'

'Sorry, ma'am!' he said. 'When I get my freedom it sort of goes to my head, don't you know. But please don't be angry; just listen to my plan.' He had flown up on top of the cage, and took hold of the cover which was hooked on to it. 'I'm going to put the cover on,' he said, as he pulled it neatly down over the cage with his beak, making it quite dark for Mrs Pepperpot inside.

'Now,' said the bird, 'Mrs Happy won't notice that you're in there instead of me. She'll want me to do my party piece to impress her precious guests, so when you hear her say: "Come on, pet, say 'Thank you, Mama' and 'Pipkins Happy',' you just tell her what you think of her.'

'But you haven't told me why you don't like her,' objected Mrs Pepperpot.

'She's mean, and for all her talk about how clever I am, she neglects me. I often have to go without fresh water or she forgets to give me any grain. But you'll soon see what she's like.' And with that Suchislife flew out of the window and hid in a tree to watch what would happen.

Mrs Pepperpot had just settled herself comfortably on the budgerigar's swing when she heard the ladies come into the sitting room.

'D'you think it can really talk?' she heard one of them say.

'Four words; think of that!' said the second lady.

'Wonderful, isn't it?' said the third lady.

Mrs Pepperpot didn't know what to do. She could hear Mrs Happy getting the tea ready in the kitchen, and now she heard the ladies coming nearer the cage.

'Shall we have a peep at it?' asked the first lady.

'D'you think we dare?' said the second.

'We could just lift the cover a little bit,' suggested the third.

But at the moment a little voice from inside the cage squeaked: 'Don't touch the cover!'

'How very strange,' said the first lady. 'It said four words exactly. Mrs Happy! Your budgie has just talked to us – we heard it clearly.'

Mrs Happy came in with the cakes; she was so taken up with getting the tea served, that she didn't ask *what* words the bird had said. She didn't even notice the cover was on.

'My Pipkins is so clever! Now do sit down all of you and make yourselves at home.' And they all sat down and started chattering the way ladies do, and Mrs Pepperpot stayed as quiet as if she had really been a budgerigar under the cover. But she listened to every word that was being said.

'I must tell you,' said Mrs Happy, laughing gaily, 'about the funny neighbour I have just down the road. She's a little old woman with long skirts and a shawl, and she wears her hair scraped back like something from Grandma's time. She's a scream! She will come tripping in here, knocking at the door . . .'

From the cage came an indignant squeak: 'You invited her yourself!'

For a moment Mrs Happy didn't know what to say, but then she laughed again: 'Isn't he funny? You'd almost think he was joining in the conversation, but, of course, he doesn't know what he's saying. I'll get him to say his name, but first I'll take the cover off so you can see him.' And she got up to do this.

'Don't touch the cover!' squeaked the voice from the cage.

'That's what it said before!' said one of the ladies.

'How very odd!' said Mrs Happy. 'Perhaps someone else has been teaching him to talk while I was out. Well, we won't bother with him just now. I was telling you about the funny old woman down the road; she has the quaintest little house . . .'

'That's not what you say when you go borrowing rhubarb and sugar and eggs and parsley and anything else you've forgotten to buy. The little old woman's good enough for that, Mrs Snobby Happy!'

All the ladies were aghast. Mrs Happy jumped up and ran to the table to snatch off the cover. But her foot slipped and she fell, knocking the whole cage out of the open window!

While the ladies screamed and picked up Mrs Happy, Suchislife flew down from the tree where he'd been hiding. He quickly unhinged the cage door and let Mrs Pepperpot out. Then he hopped in himself and Mrs Pepperpot shut the door behind him.

'Well done!' he said. 'I watched the whole performance and you certainly gave that old cat just the right medicine.'

Mrs Pepperpot was still shaking with anger. 'She won't be wanting to borrow from me again in a hurry! Of all the ungrateful, two-faced . . .' But Mrs Pepperpot didn't have time to finish her sentence because just then she grew to her normal size. She picked up the cage with Suchislife inside and knocked on the front door.

Inside there was so much noise going on that they didn't hear Mrs Pepperpot's knock, so she walked in.

What a sight! Mrs Happy was lying on the sofa, moaning and holding her head, while two of her guests were mopping up the third who had had the whole pot of tea spilt over her! They didn't seem to see Mrs Pepperpot, so she put the cage on the table and said: 'I found this in the garden. I suppose it must be the bird you were telling me about, the one that talks so well?'

'Take it away, Mrs Pepperpot, take it away!' groaned Mrs Happy. 'I never want to see it again!'

'But I thought it was the cleverest bird alive,' said Mrs Pepperpot, who could hardly keep from smiling.

'It's far too clever for me,' said Mrs Happy, 'and I'd be pleased if you would accept it as a present –

in return for all the nice things you've done for me this summer.'

'Don't mention it, Mrs Happy,' said Mrs Pepperpot, 'but I'd be glad to take Suchislife – I mean Pipkins – home, if you really don't want him any more.'

Then Mrs Pepperpot carried the cage out of the door, down the path and through the handsome wrought-iron gates, and the little blue bird just jumped up and down inside, saying one word over and over again: 'Happy, happy, happy, happy!'

'*I'm* happy too,' said Mrs Pepperpot.

# Mrs Pepperpot Turns Detective

MRS PEPPERPOT has tried her hand at many jobs, but this autumn she has tried something new – she has turned detective.

Of all the seasons Mrs Pepperpot likes autumn best. When anyone complains that it's dark and dreary, she always answers that it's the best time of the year, because then we get the reward for all the hard work we put in in the spring with our digging and sowing and planting.

'But the days get so short and the nights get so long!' they say.

'That makes it all the cosier indoors,' says Mrs Pepperpot, 'and think of all the fun the children have, playing detectives with torches in the dark.'

'All right, but what about the burglars and suchlike? They have a much better chance to do their stealing at this time of year.'

So the argument ran, but Mrs Pepperpot said no more, because you see, someone had been stealing from *her*, and she very much wanted to play detective herself.

And what d'you think was being stolen from Mrs Pepperpot? Her potatoes, of all things! Ever since September, when she first started digging them up, she had been finding plants with no potatoes under them; they had been dug up, the potatoes taken off and then the plants stuck back in the soil to make them look as if they were still growing. Wasn't that a cunning trick?

Mrs Pepperpot couldn't think who it could be. If only she were a *real* detective; then she could trace footprints in the mud, perhaps even fingerprints on the leaves of the potato plants. She could build a secret observation post and carry a gun, and when she had caught the thief red-handed, she would say: 'Hands up!'

At supper one night she was thinking so hard about being a detective that she said 'Hands up!' when she was passing a bowl of hot stew to her husband, and he dropped it all over the clean tablecloth in his fright. For once she couldn't very well scold him.

After supper she remembered she had left her potato bucket out in the field almost full of potatoes. 'I'd better fetch it in, or the thief might take that too,' she thought.

She put a scarf round her head and found the torch, for it was a very dark night. Then she went out to the field and was just bending down to pick up the bucket when she heard someone climbing through the hedge. Quickly she put out the torch and got right down on her knees over the bucket, so that she couldn't be seen.

'I'll catch him this time!' she said to herself and her heart was going pitter-pat with excitement! But was she *cross* a moment later, when she found herself sprawling among the potatoes in the bucket; she had SHRUNK, of course.

It wasn't even any good trying to climb out of the bucket; because how could she get through all that mud back to the house while she was tiny? And she did so want to catch the thief! So, there was nothing for it but to lie where she was and try and see what the thief looked like.

First she listened very carefully; there was some-one climbing through the hedge, right enough. But what was that? Two more people seemed to be coming through, and they were not being very quiet about it, either! Now she could hear them whispering to each other: 'Mind how you go!' This was a *boy's* voice.

'I had to pull him through the hedge!' answered a *girl's* voice.

'She hurt me!' wailed another younger voice.

'Ssh!' whispered the big boy, 'or we'll go straight home and not get any potatoes tonight!'

Mrs Pepperpot could hear them coming down one of the rows with a spade. They also had a bucket which rattled. The steps stopped. Now she could hear the spade going into the soil.

'Look, Sis,' said the big boy's voice, 'these are wopping great potatoes. Hold the bucket!'

The smaller child's footsteps started coming in Mrs Pepperpot's direction and in another moment he had found her bucket.

'Tum here, tum here!' he called in a high baby voice, quite forgetting he had promised to keep quiet.

'What is it?' hissed the big boy. 'Don't shout!'

But the little boy went on: 'Lots o' 'tatoes in a bucket!' he announced.

'I'll give you lots o' 'tatoes in a bucket!' muttered Mrs Pepperpot to herself; 'I'll have you all three arrested when I get back to my proper size.'

Then, as quietly as she could, she worked her way down under the top layer of potatoes, so that the children wouldn't see her. It was only just in time, as the big boy and the girl came over to have a look, and they were so pleased with little brother's find that the big boy lifted up the bucket and made for the hedge.

'You carry the other bucket,' whispered the big boy to the little one, 'it's not so heavy.'

'I dood! I dood!' piped the little fellow who couldn't say his 'k's' and 'g's'. 'I find lots o' 'tatoes!' and he scrambled after the others, dragging the lighter bucket after him.

'It's a good thing it's so dark,' said the big boy, as they all got through the hedge on to the path, 'no one can see us here.'

The girl shivered a little: 'I feel like a real burglar in a detective story,' she said.

'I burgle-burgle,' chimed in the little one.

'Burglars don't usually carry detectives around in buckets!' said Mrs Pepperpot to herself. 'Just you wait, my fine friends!'

At last the children stopped at a door. They knocked and called: 'Open the door, Mother, and see what we've brought!'

The door opened and Mrs Pepperpot heard a woman's voice say: 'My! That's a fine bucketful; it'll keep us well fed for days. I'll heat the water in the pot straight away.'

'I ha' some too!' shouted the youngest, showing her the big potatoes in his bucket.

'Two buckets! That means you've taken one that doesn't belong to us. One of you'll have to take it back when you've eaten.'

'But, Mother!' said the boy.

'There's no "but" about it,' said his mother firmly. 'We may be so poor we have to help ourselves to a few potatoes now and then, but I hope to make it up to the owner of that field before too long. The bucket goes straight back!'

Mrs Pepperpot could hardly believe her ears; here was a family right on her doorstep, so to speak, and she didn't know they were going hungry. They must be new to the neighbourhood, or surely someone would have helped them. Well, she would certainly let them have whatever potatoes they needed, no doubt about that. She had almost forgotten she was being a detective and a doll's size one at that, when the mother started lifting the potatoes out of the bucket to put them in the saucepan, which was now bubbling on the stove.

Poor Mrs Pepperpot! What should she do?

'A fine thing!' she said to herself, burrowing deeper and deeper into the bucket to hide herself. 'Here I am, being sorry for them because they're poor, when I ought to be sorry for myself, going to be boiled alive any minute now!'

At last all the potatoes were in the pot and only Mrs Pepperpot was left, but by now she was so covered in earth that the mother didn't notice her.

But the little boy did. He was peering into the bucket, and he put his small hand in and lifted Mrs Pepperpot out.

'That's torn it!' said Mrs Pepperpot and shut her eyes.

'What a funny li'l 'tato!' said the little boy. 'I teep it.' And he ran off with her into the scullery, where he hid behind the door. The rest of the family were too taken up with getting the meal ready to notice where he went.

Sitting on a box, the little boy held Mrs Pepperpot very carefully on his knee.

'You my 'tato?' he asked.

Mrs Pepperpot nodded: 'That's right. I'm your 'tato.'

The little boy's eyes grew round with amazement. 'You *talking* 'tato?' he asked.

'That's right,' said Mrs Pepperpot again. 'I'm a talking 'tato.'

'Tan I eat you?' he asked, looking at her very closely.

Mrs Pepperpot shivered a bit, but she spoke very calmly: 'I don't think I would, if I were you, sonny. I don't make very good eating.'

Just then his mother called him to eat his dinner. So he put Mrs Pepperpot down on the box and said: 'I ha' dinner now. You my talking 'tato – you stay here – I tum back soon play wi' you.'

'Well, sonny,' said Mrs Pepperpot, 'I may have to go, but I'll come back tomorrow and then I'll bring you a present. How's that?'

'You bring me 'nother talking 'tato!' he said and ran back to his mother who was putting a great heap of mashed potato on his plate.

Mrs Pepperpot wondered what she should do next. If she climbed back into the bucket and waited for a ride home in that, it might take hours before the boy went back to the field, and Mr Pepperpot would be fretting about her. Just then there was a little scratching noise behind the box and a mouse peeped out.

'Hullo,' said Mrs Pepperpot in mouse language.

The mouse came out to look at her, and Mrs Pepperpot had never seen such a skinny creature.

'If you'll help me get out of here,' she said, 'I have a nice piece of bacon at home you can have.'

The mouse pricked up its ears. 'Bacon, did you say? We haven't seen bacon in this house for a very long time.'

'Why d'you stay here if there's so little to eat?' asked Mrs Pepperpot, as she got on the mouse's back.

'Well,' said the mouse, starting off through a hole in the wall, 'I've been with the family all my life, you know, so I don't like to leave them in the lurch. I mean, what would people say if they found out there wasn't enough food here to feed a mouse?'

When they got to the foot of the hill leading to her house, Mrs Pepperpot thanked the mouse and promised to put the piece of bacon behind the box in the scullery the next day. Then she very conveniently grew large and hurried on home.

Mr Pepperpot was standing at the front door, anxiously peering out into the dark. 'Where have you been all this time?' he asked.

'Looking for my bucket of potatoes,' said Mrs Pepperpot. 'Can't you see how grubby I am? Crawling on my hands and knees in the mud I was, but I couldn't find it anywhere.'

Did the boy bring back the bucket? Did Mrs Pepperpot have the children arrested? And what about the little boy's talking 'tato? Well, all that is part of another story.

# Mrs Pepperpot and the
# Brooch Hunt


THE LAST time Mrs Pepperpot tried her hand at playing detective you may remember she nearly ended up as mashed potato. But she still has a secret longing to be one of those smart detectives you see on the films – the kind that solve everything as easy as winking.

Meanwhile, she has decided not to arrest those potato thieves. Instead, she goes to see the family almost every day and she knows all their names. There's Mrs Grey, the mother, who tries to keep the home together. It's very difficult for her, because her husband's been out of work for many months and now he's gone to the coast to see if he can get a job on a boat. Then there's Peter, who is ten and a sensible boy, and Betty, who is eight, and little Bobby, who is only three. He keeps asking about his talking potato, and, though the other children don't know what he's talking about, Mrs Pepperpot does, so she has bought him a clockwork frog to play with instead.

Each time she visits the Greys she brings some potatoes, and she doesn't forget the hungry mouse, either; he gets a bit of bacon rind behind the door in the scullery. When she goes home the children often walk part of the way with her and talk about all sorts of things.

Once she happened to say that she had lost a little silver brooch – one she had been given as a christening present.

'I hate to lose it,' she told the children, 'because I've had it all my life and it's a pretty little thing.'

'Why don't you let us be detectives and help you find it?' Peter asked.

'Oh yes!' cried Betty, clapping her hands. 'That would be fun!'

'*I* want to be deti-deti too!' shouted Bobby, dancing up and down.

'Oh, it's hardly worth making too much fuss about,' said Mrs Pepperpot, though she secretly rather liked the idea.

'Come on, Mrs Pepperpot,' said Peter, putting on a grown-up detective sort of voice, 'tell us where you last remember seeing the lost item.'

Mrs Pepperpot smiled: 'Now, let me see; I think I wore it at Nelly North's when we had a club meeting there last month.'

Peter got out a piece of paper and pencil and noted this down.

'Right,' he said, 'when can we start investigations?'

'Well,' said Mrs Pepperpot, 'I'm busy all day tomorrow with the washing, but we could meet here about four o'clock, and by then I may have thought where else I might have left it.'

'And we can work out a plan of campaign,' said Peter importantly.

So the children promised to meet Mrs Pepperpot by a certain big fir tree on the road between their house and hers at four o'clock the next day, and they were very excited about it, especially little Bobby, who kept talking about the deti-detis till his mother put him to bed.

Next day at four o'clock sharp they all met at the tree. Mrs Pepperpot had brought a torch, because it got dark so early.

'First we'll walk over the meadow to Nelly North's farm,' she said. 'I have an idea it might be under her sofa. She's not a very tidy person, but I don't want to offend her by hinting she hasn't cleaned her room properly, so I want you, Peter, to take this torch and shine it under the sofa while I keep Nelly talking. You must do it secretly, mind, so that she doesn't notice.'

'What about Bobby and me?' asked Betty.

'You'll have to keep watch outside,' said Mrs Pepperpot.

So they started off across the meadow, walking in single file along a narrow path with Mrs Pepperpot in front, shining the torch. Suddenly the torch flew up in the air and Mrs Pepperpot disappeared! At least, that's what the children thought, for, of course, *we* know that she had shrunk again! The torch was still alight when it landed, but Mrs Pepperpot had rolled into the long grass, and it was Bobby who found her and picked her up by one leg!

'Here's my talking 'tato!' he shouted, dangling poor Mrs Pepperpot upside down.

'Put it down, Bobby,' said Betty, 'it might bite!'

'No!' insisted Bobby, who had now set Mrs Pepperpot on his hand. 'It's my talking 'tato!'

Mrs Pepperpot had now got her breath back, so she said as quietly as she could: 'That's right, children, Bobby *has* seen me like this before.'

'Why, it's Mrs Pepperpot!' cried Peter and Betty together. 'However did you get so small?'

'That will take too long to explain,' said Mrs Pepperpot, 'but it happens to me from time to time, and last time Bobby found me in the bottom of the potato bucket, so that's why he thinks I'm a talking potato.'

'Let *me* hold you,' said Betty. 'I'll be very careful.'

'Yes, I think I would feel a bit safer,' said Mrs Pepperpot, as Bobby was jogging her up and down in his excitement, making her quite giddy.

'What about our search? Will we have to call it off?' asked Peter.

Mrs Pepperpot didn't like to disappoint them, and she'd already thought up a new plan, but first she made them promise never to tell anybody about her turning small.

'You must hold up your right hands, as they do in the films, and swear you will never speak of this to a living soul.'

Peter and Betty held up their right hands and repeated Mrs Pepperpot's words, but little Bobby had to be told he would get a hard smack if he ever said he'd seen a talking potato!

'Now,' said Mrs Pepperpot, 'instead of me going in to talk to Nelly North, I want Peter to knock at the door. When Nelly opens it he must say that he's collecting for – let's see – a home for worn-out car tyres. If he says it quickly she won't notice, and then when she's gone to the kitchen to look for a penny, you just switch on the torch and shine it under the sofa in the front room, and if you see a shining object, bring it with you. Betty and Bobby and I will be waiting behind that tree over there.'

By now they had reached the road in front of North Farm and Mrs Pepperpot pointed her tiny hand at a tree standing a little way from the house.

'Right oh!' said Peter and walked bravely over to the door, hiding the torch in his pocket.

The others waited in the dark till he came back. It didn't take long, but Peter was quite excited when he came towards them, and he was holding something in his hand.

'Let me see!' said Mrs Pepperpot, who was standing on Betty's hand. Peter put the object down beside her and shone the torch on it.

'Oh dear!' she said, 'I'm afraid you've picked up the wrong thing. This is a silver ring that was sent to Nelly from her uncle in America; she said she had lost it the day of the meeting.'

Peter's face had fallen. 'What do we do now?'

'It's no good going back, you would find it too hard to explain,' said Mrs Pepperpot. 'Put it in your pocket while we go on to Sally South's house just along the road here. That's another place I think I may have dropped my brooch when I was there for the silver wedding party.'

So they walked on to Sally South's house, Mrs Pepperpot riding in Betty's pocket and Bobby kept putting his fingers in to see if she was still there.

Sally didn't know Peter when she opened the door to him, and she was a bit deaf, so she didn't quite catch what he was collecting for, but he looked a nice boy, so she went off for a penny from her money box. While she was out of the room Peter got the chance to shine his torch under the furniture and even behind the grandfather cloth. There he saw something glittering, so he fished it out and put it in his pocket. When Sally came back he thanked her very nicely for the penny and ran back to the others who were hiding outside.

'Did you find it?' whispered Betty.

'I think so,' said Peter, bringing the little thing out of his pocket.

But when she saw it Mrs Pepperpot shook her head; 'Sorry, Peter, I'm afraid that's not it either. It's a medallion Sally's husband gave her for a silver wedding present. He was very cross when he found she had dropped it that day.'

Peter looked quite disheartened. 'This doesn't seem such a good idea, after all,' he said. 'Perhaps we'd better give it up.'

'Is that the way for Detective Sergeant Peter Grey to speak?' demanded Mrs Pepperpot, who was really enjoying the hunt, though it was true she wasn't doing the hard work! 'Let's try East Farm; Mr Pepperpot and I were there just after Christmas for the baby's christening. I was godmother, so I carried the baby, and I expect the brooch fell off when I was putting the baby in his cot.'

'Can I carry my talking 'tato now?' asked Bobby who had been very good and quiet for a long time.

'All right, but don't you drop me now,' said Mrs Pepperpot, whose clothes and hair were getting quite messed up with all this passing from hand to hand.

When they got to East Farm only Mr East was at home, looking after the baby. He was a kindly man and never minded giving children the odd penny. So he put down his newspaper and went out to search for a coin in his jacket pocket. The baby was lying in a cot, playing with his toes. Peter remembered what Mrs Pepperpot had said about putting the baby in his cot, so when he saw a small silver bell in the cot beside the baby, he quickly picked it up and pocketed it. Mr East came in and gave him the penny, and Peter thanked him politely and ran out to the others.

'I hope I've got the right thing this time!' he cried, jingling the little bell as he pulled it out of his pocket.

'Oh, you silly boy!' exclaimed Mrs Pepperpot, 'how could you think that was my brooch? It belongs to the baby's rattle which I gave him myself for a christening present!'

Peter looked very sheepish; 'Well, you see, I don't really know what a brooch *is*!'

'Why didn't you say so before?' Mrs Pepperpot was beginning to get cross. 'A detective needs to know what he's looking for!'

'*I* know what a brooch is,' said Betty, 'it has a pin which fits into a clasp and you put it in your shawl.'

'That's right,' said Mrs Pepperpot, who was trying hard to think where else they could search. 'I've got it. I'm sure I wore it for Paul West's confirmation. It was pouring with rain that day and I took my umbrella; I bet it dropped into the umbrella stand at West Farm. Come along, children, if it isn't there we'll go home, I promise you.'

So they turned about and trudged down a little lane till they got to West Farm. Peter knocked, as before, but this time there was no answer, so he tried the handle and the door opened. There, just inside, was the umbrella stand Mrs Pepperpot had told him about, so he quickly shone his torch right down to the bottom of it, and, Goodness Gracious! there he could see a small pin with what looked like the letter 'P' on it! Surely that must be it, thought Peter and made a dive for it. Then he ran out to the others, hoping no one had heard him.

This time they were hiding behind a shed and Peter made sure he was out of sight of the house before he opened his hand: 'There,' he said, 'I've got it!'

'Show me,' said Mrs Pepperpot, but then she almost cried: 'This isn't my brooch – it's a tie pin!'

'But it had "P" on it, so I thought it must be Pepperpot!' stammered poor Peter.

'I wasn't *christened* Pepperpot, was I? I only married him! The "P" stands for Paul who was confirmed that day. Goodness, how careless everybody is with their belongings!'

There was nothing for it now; they would have to give up and go home. What bothered Mrs Pepperpot was how to return all those things to their rightful owners. For once she really hadn't been very clever.

The three children were tired and walking slowly along the road, Betty holding Mrs Pepperpot, when suddenly they heard running footsteps coming in their direction.

'They're after us!' squeaked Mrs Pepperpot. 'Run, children!'

In their fright the children nearly fell over each other and poor Mrs Pepperpot was thrown right over the ditch into the field.

The footsteps were coming nearer.

'Stop thief!' shouted someone. It was Nelly North. 'I can see them.'

'There's the boy!' shouted Sally South who was following her.

Mr East was plodding behind with fat Mrs West. 'Come on, boy,' he shouted, 'you might as well give up!'

The children were crying by now and little Bobby stumbled over a stone and fell.

At that moment a small but commanding voice came through the air. 'Hands up or I shoot!' it shouted. It seemed to be coming from nowhere and everyone stood stock still. Then it spoke again: 'This

is the secret police calling with a message for the following people: Mrs North, Mrs South, Mr East and Mrs West. Stand by please! Can you hear me?'

They were all so surprised to hear their name called, that they very meekly answered, 'Yes.'

'Right,' went on the voice. 'You can all expect a surprise in your letter boxes tomorrow morning. On one condition, that you immediately go home and leave the children alone!'

The children had stopped running too, and watched with amazement as, one by one, Nelly North, Sally South, Mr East and fat Mrs West all turned about and walked away without a single look behind them.

'Phew!' said a voice right beside the children. There stood Mrs Pepperpot, as large as life, She was holding a dock leaf in her hand and it was curled in the shape of a large cone.

'What's that for?' asked little Bobby who had

picked himself up and was *very* pleased to see his friend Mrs Pepperpot again.

'The secret police always carry loudspeakers!' she answered, smiling at the children. Then they all went home to her house and had nice hot cocoa and pancakes.

Next morning when Nelly North looked in her letter box she found the silver ring she had lost, Sally South found her silver medallion, Mr East found the silver bell from the baby's rattle and Mrs West found her son's tie pin. They certainly were surprised!

But the one who was most surprised was Mrs Pepperpot. When she opened *her* letter-box she found a little parcel in it, and inside was her brooch. There was also a note from Peter, which said:

*Dear Mrs Pepperpot,*

*After the clue you gave us last night, your detectives have been able to solve the mystery. We have put your potato bucket back in its place in the potato field. Thank you.*

*Yours truly,*
*Detective Sergeant P. Grey*

'Of course!' said Mrs Pepperpot to herself, 'I was wearing the brooch on the night when the potato thieves came, and I must have dropped it in the bucket!'

# The Ski Race

MRS PEPPERPOT has done a lot of things in her life and most of them I've told you about already. But now I must tell you how she went ski racing one day last winter.

Mr Pepperpot had decided to go in for the annual local ski race. He had been a pretty good skier when he was young, so he said to Mrs Pepperpot:

'I don't see why I shouldn't have a go this year; I feel more fit than I have for many years.'

'That's right, husband, you do that,' said Mrs Pepperpot, 'and if you win the cup you'll get your favourite ginger cake when you come home.'

So Mr Pepperpot put his name down, and when the day came he put on his white anorak and blue cap with a bobble on the top and strings under his chin. He slung his skis over his shoulders and said he would wax them when he got to the starting point.

'Righto! Best of luck!' said Mrs Pepperpot. She was already greasing the cake tin and stoking the stove for her baking.

'Thanks, wife,' said Mr Pepperpot and went off. It was not before he had turned the corner by the main road that Mrs Pepperpot caught sight of his tin of wax, which he had left on the sideboard.

'What a dunderhead that man is!' exclaimed Mrs Pepperpot. 'Now I shall have to go after him, I suppose; otherwise his precious skis are more likely to go backwards than forwards and there'll be no cup in this house today.'

So Mrs Pepperpot flung her shawl round her shoulders and trotted up the road as fast as she could with the tin of wax. When she got near the starting point there was a great crowd gathered. She dodged in and out to try and find her husband, but everyone seemed to be wearing white anoraks and blue caps. At last she saw a pair of sticks

237

stuck in the snow with a blue cap hanging from the top. She could see the initials P.P. sewn in red thread inside.

'That must be his cap,' thought Mrs Pepperpot. 'Those are his initials, Peter Pepperpot. I sewed them on myself in red thread like that. I'll just drop the wax in the cap; then he'll find it when he comes to pick up his sticks.'

As she bent forward to put the wax in the cap she accidentally knocked it off the stick and at

that moment she shrank so quickly that it was *she* who fell into the cap, while the tin of wax rolled out into the snow!

'No harm done,' thought Mrs Pepperpot; 'when he comes along he'll see me in his cap. Then he can put me down somewhere out of the way of the race. And as soon as I grow large again I can go home.'

But a moment later a big hand reached down, snatched up the cap and crammed it over a mop of thick hair. The strings were firmly tied and Mrs Pepperpot was trapped!

'Oh well!' she thought. 'I'd better not say anything before the race starts.' For she knew Mr Pepperpot hated to think anybody might get to know about her shrinking.

'Number 46!' she heard the starter shout, 'on your mark, get set, go!' And Number 46, with Mrs Pepperpot in his cap, glided off to a smooth start.

'Somebody must have lent him some wax,' she thought; 'there's nothing wrong with his skis, anyway.' Then from under the cap she shouted, 'Don't overdo it, now, or you'll have no breath left for the spurt at the end!'

She could feel the skier slow up a little. 'I suppose you know who's under your cap?' she added. 'You had forgotten the wax, so I brought it along. Only I fell into your cap instead of the wax.'

Mrs Pepperpot now felt the skier's head turn round to see if anyone was talking to him from behind.

'It's me, you fool!' said Mrs Pepperpot. 'I've shrunk again. You'll have to put me off by the lane to our house – you pass right by, remember?'

But the skier had stopped completely now.

'Come on, man, get a move on!' shouted Mrs Pepperpot. 'They'll all be passing you!'

'Is it . . . is it true that you're the little old woman who shrinks to the size of a pepperpot?'

'Of course – you know that!' laughed Mrs Pepperpot.

'Am *I* married to *you*? Is it *my* wife who shrinks?'

'Yes, yes, but hurry now!'

'No,' said the skier, 'if that's how it is I'm not going on with the race at all.'

'Rubbish!' shouted Mrs Pepperpot. 'You *must* go on! I put a cake in the oven before I went out and if it's scorched it'll be all your fault!'

But the skier didn't budge.

'Maybe you'd like me to pop out of your cap and show myself to everybody? Any minute now

I might go back to my full size and then the cap will burst and the whole crowd will see who is married to the shrinking woman. Come on, now! With any luck you may just do it, but there's no time to lose; HURRY!'

This worked; the skier shot off at full speed, helping himself to huge strides with his sticks. 'Fore!' he shouted as he sped past the other skiers. But when they came to the refreshment stall Mrs Pepperpot could smell the lovely hot soup, and she thought her husband deserved a break. 'We're well up now,' she called. 'You could take a rest.'

The skier slowed down to a stop and Mrs Pepperpot could hear there were many people standing round him. 'Well done!' they said. 'You're very well placed. But what are you looking

so worried about? Surely you're not frightened of the last lap, are you?'

'No, no, nothing like that!' said the skier. 'It's this cap of mine – I'm dead scared of my cap!'

But the people patted him on the back and told him not to worry, he had a good chance of winning.

Under the cap Mrs Pepperpot was getting restless again. 'That's enough of that!' she called. 'We'll have to get on now!'

The people who stood nearest heard the voice and wondered who spoke. The woman who ladled out the soup said, 'Probably some loud speaker.'

And Mrs Pepperpot couldn't help laughing. 'Nearer the truth than you think!' she thought. Then she called out again, 'Come on, husband, put that spurt on, and let's see if we can make it!'

And the skis shot away again, leaping many yards each time the sticks struck into the snow. Very soon Mrs Pepperpot could hear the sound of clapping and cheering.

'What do we do now?' whispered the skier in a miserable voice. 'Can you last another minute? Then I can throw the cap off under the fir trees just before we reach the finishing line.'

'Yes, that will be all right,' said Mrs Pepperpot. And, as the skis sped down the last slope, the strings were untied and the cap flew through the air, landing safely under the fir trees.

When Mrs Pepperpot had rolled over and over many times she found herself growing big once more. So she got up, shook the snow off her skirt and walked quietly home to her house. From the cheering in the distance she was sure her husband had won the cup.

The cake was only a little bit burnt on the top when she took it out of the oven, so she cut off the black part and gave it to the cat. Then she whipped some cream to put on top and made a steaming pot of coffee to have ready for her champion husband.

Sure enough, Mr Pepperpot soon came home – *without* the cup. 'I forgot to take the wax,' he said, 'so I didn't think it was worth going in for the race. But I watched it, and you should have seen Paul Petersen today; I've never seen him run like that in all my born days. All the same, he looked very queer, as if he'd seen a ghost or something. When it was over he kept talking about his wife and his cap, and he wasn't satisfied till he'd telephoned his house and made sure his wife had been there all the time, watching the race on television.'

Then Mrs Pepperpot began to laugh. And ever since, when she's feeling sad or things are not going just right, all she has to do is to remember the day she went ski racing in the wrong cap, and then she laughs and laughs and laughs.

# It all started with a Scarecrow

**Puffin is over seventy years old.**
Sounds ancient, doesn't it? But Puffin has never been
so lively. We're always on the lookout for the next big
idea, which is how it began all those years ago.

Penguin Books was a big idea from the mind of
a man called Allen Lane, who in 1935 invented
the quality paperback and changed the world.
**And from great Penguins, great Puffins grew,
changing the face of children's books forever.**

The first four Puffin Picture Books were hatched in 1940 and the
first Puffin story book featured a man with broomstick arms called
Worzel Gummidge. In 1967 Kaye Webb, Puffin Editor, started the
Puffin Club, promising to **'make children into readers'**.
She kept that promise and over 200,000 children became devoted
Puffineers through their quarterly instalments of *Puffin Post*.

Many years from now, we hope you'll look back and
remember Puffin with a smile. **No matter what your age
or what you're into, there's a Puffin for everyone.**
The possibilities are endless, but one thing is for sure:
whether it's a picture book or a paperback, a sticker book
or a hardback. **if it's got that little Puffin
on it – it's bound to be good.**

A Puffin Book can take you to amazing places.

# WHERE WILL YOU GO?

## #PackAPuffin